Percy runs throu̲̲̲̲̲̲̲̲̲̲̲̲̲̲̲̲̲̲̲ .... noke number, time spotted, bearing . . . colour of smoke. . . . When she finishes, she watches through her binoculars and waits, her mind turning to Gilmore. He sounded friendly and helpful, called her by her name; but has he read her message? Nothing in his voice suggested that he had, but then again, how would she know?

She keeps her binoculars focused on the smoke. Now that the helicopter has located the fire, she will relay messages from ground to air, if needed. Her adrenaline high subsides, and she feels a familiar vulnerability. Always there is this same letdown after a smoke, the excitement gone, and her role, so momentarily crucial, diminished once more. . . .

She starts down the ladder . . . Now that they've found the smoke, the men will work well into the night. . . . If they need her, she will be here. She may cry between calls, may wrap her arms around herself and rock in place, may whimper like a baby, but no one will know.

PEARL LUKE spent summers working in Canadian fire towers while completing her master's degree in English literature. Her short fiction and essays have been published in several literary magazines and anthologies, and she is a regular contributor to the *Calgary Herald*. She lives in Calgary, Alberta, and on Vancouver Island, British Columbia.

Burning Ground

Pearl Luke

A PLUME BOOK

For Robert, Amanda, Breanne, and Austin, with love

PLUME
Published by the Penguin Group
Penguin Putnam Inc., 375 Hudson Street, New York, New York 10014, U.S.A.
Penguin Books Ltd, 27 Wrights Lane, London W8 5TZ, England
Penguin Books Australia Ltd, Ringwood, Victoria, Australia
Penguin Books Canada Ltd, 10 Alcorn Avenue, Toronto, Ontario, Canada M4V 3B2
Penguin Books (N.Z.) Ltd, 182–190 Wairau Road, Auckland 10, New Zealand

Penguin Books Ltd, Registered Offices: Harmondsworth, Middlesex, England

Published by Plume, a member of Penguin Putnam Inc.

First American Printing, September 2001
10 9 8 7 6 5 4 3 2 1

℗ REGISTERED TRADEMARK—MARCA REGISTRADA

LIBRARY OF CONGRESS CATALOGING-IN-PUBLICATION DATA
Luke, Pearl.
Burning ground / Pearl Luke.
p. cm.
ISBN 0-452-28267-5 (pbk.)
1. Forest rangers—Fiction. 2. Wilderness areas—Fiction. 3. Forest fires—Fiction
4. Young women—Fiction 5. Canada—Fiction. I. Title.
PR9199.3.L84 B87 2001
813'.6—dc21   2001021022

Printed in the United States of America
Set in Aldus

PUBLISHER'S NOTE
This is a work of fiction. Names, characters, places, and incidents are either
the product of the author's imagination or are used fictitiously, and any
resemblance to actual persons, living or dead, business establishments,
events, or locales is entirely coincidental.

Prologue

SOME fires smoulder all winter in a subterranean world of roots, moss, and leaves, their flames held underground by layers of sodden, sometimes frozen, debris. Even as they burrow into the earth, each fiery offshoot sustains itself in muskeg, subsists on peat moss too light to hold water, on air pockets split like cells.

Some fires advance through coal veins, only centimetres at a time, warming the surface of the earth from the inside out. Others light spontaneously, or start when lightning stabs deep into the ground to ignite layers of dead leaves with one quick strike. Yet others begin when lightning hits the heart of a tree determined to burn from core to roots like an oversized wick. On occasion, the cause is an earlier surface fire too hastily extinguished by fatigued workers who turned soil in shallow scoops, who smothered embers but failed to expose flames pursuing roots to their farthest ends. Those are the flames that strain backward, forward, and upward again, moving any direction at all, incinerating at will until layers of wet duff turn damp, then dry, then ignite through to the surface.

Only eventually will a tentative wisp of smoke curl upward, the freed tendril forming a smallish puff. Then one or two more will appear on the horizon, testing until, as each hungry flame candles ever higher in the trees, smoke curls and writhes, twists skyward into columns of dense rolling white, violent grey, rising. If it goes unnoticed, the fire takes hold, and columns settle into uneasy layers, drift with the wind from Alberta to Manitoba, from the Territories to Quebec, until soon the length of the country is spanned by a hazy stratum coloured with whatever has been stripped from the earth—white if the fire catches in grass or pine; light grey if it burns in the snag of a dead tree or in white spruce; dark grey if the fuel is black spruce or muskeg. The thickest, blackest smoke reflects civilization—a flare, a stack, rubber from old tires, or waste in the nearest dump.

One

AT Envy River Tower, civilization is miles away. Without a generator, there would be no light, no radio, no contact, and it is here, deep in the northern Alberta forest, that Percy Turner lives alone from April to September. The tower site contains her cabin, a generator shed, an outhouse, and a hundred-foot tower she must climb every day, several times a day. Atop the tower is the cupola where she spends much of her time, vigilant, ever alert for the thinnest scar of smoke on the horizon.

Except this year, there is a difference. So long as the generator runs, so long as electricity flows and her cell phone holds a charge, she can use her computer, make and receive calls, fax, e-mail, even connect to the World Wide Web if she wants to. Onto this forested site, where the toilet is still an outhouse, where the only tap curves from a rain barrel below the eaves, she has imported an electronic microcosm that will suspend the isolation of previous years.

Already she sits hunched and fretful over her keyboard, composing e-mail to a man she has never seen. *May 25*, she keys into the upper-left corner of her screen. Then, *Dear Gilmore.*

I hope you don't mind that I filched your e-mail address when you gave it out on the radio. Although we haven't talked, I hear you several times a day.

I'm attracted to voices—much more here than anywhere else—and yours compels me to write. I can't explain, except that your voice enters my ears and filters through my body like music.

Fair enough. For Percy, who is almost thirty and old

5

enough to consider such things, there is an indescribable pull to each word that Gilmore says. She knows only that she feels, as much as hears, distinct and variable notes resonating in her spine for several seconds after he speaks. The resultant goose bumps are the reason she writes.

Nevertheless, she hesitates. Who knows what kind of trouble she invites, saying something so provocative to a complete stranger? The very act of writing seems dangerous, irresponsible, not something she would normally do.

Then again, how much trouble could he cause? It's not as if he can drop in unannounced, follow her home, park down the street, watch her windows in the dark. He's safer than that. Miles away safe. Setting her chin slightly, she adds:

In fact, voice takes on a whole new significance at a tower, don't you think?

What Percy means is that everything takes on new significance at the fire tower. Newspapers and groceries, flown in once a month, are like gifts. She must buy them herself, but she prefers to think of them as presents from benevolent forestry workers who may, if she's been grateful enough in the past, remember to buy some of her fruit ripe, some green, some turning, so that she need not gobble everything at once before it rots.

Have you been working on towers long? This is my seventh year, but each year the solitude gets harder to manage. Every fall, when the season ends, I tell myself I'm never coming back, but somehow, every spring, I find myself here again. I don't like climbing the ladder five or six times a day either, but it's one way to keep my muscles tight.

I just wanted to let you know that you have a neighbour on the Internet. If you write back, I'll respond same day. How on that?

How on that? Percy hesitates over the phrase. However

useful this question is on the radio, she's not sure that it works here. She moves the cursor up and deletes. She'd rather be too earnest than ridiculous.

Sincerely, Percy Turner (668)

That Gilmore knows her by name, Percy doesn't doubt. There was a time when she could hear ten or twelve others, but a newer, more site-specific system has isolated each tower. When there are only four or five voices within hearing range, one makes a point of knowing whom one hears.

He'll write, Percy says, and her voice startles her. Until she spoke, only the whirr of the computer fan and the gentle putt-putt of the generator broke the stillness. She shrinks a little at the sound, resettles into her own silence. He'll be flattered. He'll jump at a chance for communication, for more than what can be said on a district radio. Anyone would.

SHE first heard his voice the day he arrived at Weldon Lake, only a few days after she opened at Envy River.

XMB four-five, this is XMA six-four-nine with an opening message.

Six-four-nine, this is four-five. Go ahead.

To XMB four-five. Message number one. On April twenty-third at fourteen-twenty, Weldon Lake Tower is officially open for the current fire season. Propane at nine-five percent. Onan generator set—propane—reading one-four-three-nine-three decimal two-five. Signed, Gilmore Graham. How on that?

Then, this morning, as she waited to report her morning weather, the first task of every day, she noticed just how consequential Gilmore's voice had become. After more than a month of listening, she caught herself drumming her fingers on the desk as she waited through the others. She smiled when she noticed her impatience, the fatuous smile of someone already half-smitten by the sound of morning weather off Gilmore Graham's tongue.

Four-five, this is six-four-nine with the morning weather. Max temp sixteen degrees, that's one-six, minimum seven, sky broken, visibility three-five kilometres in haze, dry bulb one-two degrees, wet bulb one-zero. Wind from the south-east at one-five kilometres, gusting three-five, rain zero decimal four millimetres. Clouds high two, middle three. Remarks thunder PM.

Or could it be that voice is to ear what pheromones are to nose? She imagines pink nerve endings waving upward, like tiny hairs, while sound waves pass over them, causing them to swell and rub together until they release endorphins that somehow signal an increase in sensory pleasure. She jots a note to herself: *Look up voice, effect of.*

Her cell phone is already plugged into the computer, so she double-clicks on Dial. In less than two minutes she has connected with the server and transferred her message into the system.

She throws a jacket over her sweater and makes a quick trip to the outhouse. The night is damp and fragrant with the green scent of cut grass, yet to Percy, it is sinister as well. She pulls her jacket close and huddles into herself while her ears and eyes strain for creatures that rustle out of sight. In another month, thankfully, it won't get dark at all. Some people hate the constancy of a northern summer's light, but she'd live in the halo of the sun all year if she could.

When she returns, chilled and shaking, she lowers a dipper into a plastic bucket of rainwater and lifts it to her lips. A quick touch to the kettle on the stove tells her that it is still warm. She heats her palms on the swollen aluminum belly, then pours only enough water in a washbowl to dunk her faded washcloth. Tomorrow, before the helicopter arrives, she will shower.

Percy and Gilmore. She moves the names past her lips, and for the first time in several hours, she thinks of Marlea. Her message to Gilmore is gone, and it's too late to change a thing.

ONLY moments ago, midway through a bowl of soup, Percy passed the afternoon weather to the radio operator. Passed. She thinks nothing of the terminology now, but there was a time when the words sounded foreign and silly. *I'm going to pass the weather.* As if the list of numbers were a kidney stone, or something swallowed and later deposited into a stainless steel bedpan at a nurse's urging.

Now her radio flares back to life as the approaching pilot calls headquarters. She had expected more warning. Usually he calls when he is farther away—just after he has begun a long final descent to her tower, a long final, as he calls it—but this time he has waited until he is almost at her tower before reporting his location.

Four-five, this is MCJ.

MCJ, this is four-five. Go ahead.

Check us on a short final for Envy River Tower.

That's copied. Short final for Envy River Tower. Four-five clear.

MCJ.

Timid at the best of times, the groundhog that lives under Percy's cabin has been cautiously nibbling stems at the edge of the forest, well-fed cheeks bulging and subsiding in anxious rhythm. Now it scuttles for the opening below the step. Whack, thump. The stubby brown tail disappears.

Seconds later, grass shudders and flattens for yards around, the underside of each blade quivering silver as the helicopter swoops over the trees, hovers, and finally settles. The pilot waits while the engine shuts down, and Percy uses the delay to check her reflection in the mirror. Her cheeks are flushed; her hair and eyes shine. Normally, unless a hunter stumbles upon her cabin, this delivery of her monthly grocery service is her only human contact.

The helicopter blades slow to a lazy circling, and the pilot and a forest ranger jump to the ground and begin to unload—several boxes of groceries, gas for the lawn mower, parcels, mail, four five-gallon buckets of water. Percy walks out to meet them.

We'll get these things, the ranger says. He's dressed in forestry attire, and streaks of perspiration run from sideburns to jawline. From beneath the brown cap, a drop runs down an escaping bristle of hair, and Percy watches it fall, sees the darker spot where it lands on his tan, crested sleeve. She has never understood why their clothes are polyester, or why the cut of the brown slacks is so tight, the shirt so fitted. No wonder they all sweat so much.

Here's your mail, the ranger says. He's old for a ranger, middle-aged and calm, not in such a rush as some of the younger ones.

Percy takes the bag gratefully and immediately delves into it. Some letters along with the bills, she says. That's what I like to see.

Now that the men are here, she practically bounces between them. If she could see herself, she'd think she looks a bit like a puppy reunited with its owner. As she walks and spins, she checks her bundle of mail, fumbling with small parcels from friends on other towers, a too-thick flip of bills, four or five personal letters—two from Marlea—and a couple of postcards. Even her acquaintances respond to loneliness.

Have you had any smokes yet?

Percy doesn't answer. She barely hears. Just seeing the letters from Marlea makes her hands shake and her head feel light. She needs a moment, but the question rests there, a faint echo in the back of her mind.

She looks from one to the other. Smokes? Did you ask if I'd seen any smokes?

The two men exchange a glance before the ranger winks. I guess we should know better than to think we can compete with your mail, he says.

Percy laughs, as if what he has said is extraordinarily witty. Unlike her usual low laughter, the sound she makes is giddy and high-pitched. Don't worry, you compete, she says. If it walks upright and it talks, I'm happy to see it.

Sounds familiar, the ranger says. Anything that moves, then?

Anything that's warm, *wet*, and moves, corrects the pilot.

At home, Percy would walk away from such crude innuendo, but she is accustomed to hearing this kind of talk from the people who stop at her tower. Some of the guys in forestry think that all tower-women go out of their minds with desire. Sometimes she's certain that she will.

Well, she says, elongating the word, filling it, as if there is more she might say but has chosen to keep it to herself. This is an all-purpose response she picked up as a child from her mother, although if she were aware that the habit came from her mother, she would rather stand stupid and speechless than use it again. She turns to the ranger, whom she has known longer than the pilot. Give me your hand, she demands.

The ranger carries a box, and his skin is still shiny with sweat. His eyes crinkle with amusement, but he pulls his elbows into his body and shakes his head.

No, really, just give me your hand.

Will it hurt? He stops by the propane tank and sets the box on the concrete pad. He makes a show of it, but he extends his hand.

Percy lays her mail on the ground and clamps her fingers around his wrist. Except for a few bird whistles and the wind rattling through poplar and spruce, all is quiet. Both men watch, wait to see what she will do next. Quickly, before he can guess, she spits a frothy white wad into the ranger's palm.

His jaw drops, and Percy, who is watching his face closely, laughs aloud.

What the hell? The ranger holds his hand, palm up, away from his body. He swivels his head, and to Percy he looks like the groundhog that just ran for cover. From the expression on his face, an observer might think his hand contained something more than a quarter teaspoon of saliva.

It's warm, says Percy. It's wet. And if you jiggle your hand a bit, it even moves. Doesn't it work for you?

The pilot flushes red when he laughs. The ranger jiggles his hand, looks into it, and thrusts it toward Percy. That's disgusting. What should I do with this?

Percy angles her shoulder toward him. You should see your face. She tries not to laugh, but she can't help herself. It's just spit. Here, wipe it on my jacket. She must stop laughing. If she doesn't, she will cry.

He wipes the bulk of it on her sleeve. Disgusting, he says again.

Like what you said wasn't? she asks, wondering how it is that for all her forced playfulness, she feels lonelier in their presence than before they arrived.

It wasn't even me. He started it. The ranger points at the pilot but smiles good-naturedly. Spit on him next time.

WHEN she first saw the letters from Marlea, Percy wanted nothing more than to rip them open. Now she treats the envelopes like junk mail, first pushes them aside, then deliberately throws them in a drawer as if she has no interest in them. She reads the postcards from her friends, and relishes each of the other letters, reading slowly, even laughing as the writers must have intended her to laugh.

When she is finished, she checks her watch and does a double take. Several hours have passed since her last tower check. She grabs her gloves and runs to the bottom of the tower. As fast as she can, she climbs, metal and cables rattling and banging. As she ascends, she counts the rungs: twenty-three, twenty-four, twenty-five ... eighty-six, eighty-seven ... ninety-nine, one hundred.

In the cupola, her chest heaves with the effort of the climb. She surveys the area around the tower with bare eyes—a full 360-degree turn. Nothing but treetops as far as she can see. There are a few shiny spots, distant lakes and swamps looking more like worn patches than actual lakes, but for the most part only vibrant green, in as many shades as one can imagine. Sometimes she thinks she has never seen anything so beautiful, so rich and thick, as the forest top spreading over the land, years old, like a fine Persian carpet protecting the earth. With binoculars, she searches the horizon again.

A white dot in the east stops her breath altogether. Damn. Can't be. She lowers the binoculars and the dot disappears, raises them, and there it is again. Smoke. Not brownish road dust, not a puff of pollen, but smoke curling skyward just this side of the far ridge, about twenty-five kilometres to the east. Percy takes deep breaths to regain her voice—the climb always loosens things up, leaves her rattling and croaking as if she had never quit smoking. She swings the scope on the fire-finder until she locates the tiny plume.

Speaking to herself, Percy practises the call. Four-five, this is six-six-eight. She clears her throat, tries to sound less clogged. Four-five. Four-five. This is six-six-eight. Six-six-eight. Got a smoke here. Got a *smoke* here. She forces her voice lower. Got a smoke. Got a smoke. She coughs, clears her throat, tries again. Gotta gotta gotta smoke. Got a smoke here. Finally, her voice holds.

Bearings in degrees mark the brass ring below the scope, and Percy jots these numbers on a slip of paper. Ninety-three degrees, forty minutes. Approximately twenty-five kilometres, she estimates. Time: 16:38. She fumbles through the drawer for the actual smoke report form, spots one pink corner and pulls the pad free. The permanent smoke record catches her eye. This is her list of all the controlled smokes that happen on a regular basis—landfill sites, oil-field batteries, flare pits, or stacks. In case she has forgotten about one of them, she grabs that as well.

Before she can check for permanent smokes, she needs an approximate location. She runs a string outward from the location of her tower on the map, conscious always of each minute ticking by. If the fire is more than .02 hectares when they reach it, she should have spotted it sooner. But how many inches equals twenty-five kilometres?

She checks her conversion chart—the map is scaled in inches, four miles to an inch, and she hasn't a clue. In elementary school, she was taught miles; by junior high, every road sign in the country had been changed to kilo-metres. Now neither of them mean anything to her. When people ask, she tells them the time. How far is it? I don't know, about forty-five minutes north, maybe fifty.

But her job requires that she estimate in either kilometres or miles, so she has markers above all the windows. Gulf flare: 15 kilometres. Bare spot: 8. Far ridge: 25. She runs her finger down the chart. Three and three-quarter inches equals twenty-four kilometres. She measures three and three-quarter inches, hesitates, and adds one line on the ruler. There. She notes the approximate section, township, and range, then flips through the record of permanent smokes looking for a similar location. When she sees nothing listed, she keys the handset on her radio.

Six-four-nine, this is six-six-eight. Percy makes the call, then peers through her binoculars. She waits a couple of seconds, then tries again.

Six-four-nine, this is six-six-eight. Are you by, Gilmore?

Six-six-eight, this is six-four-nine.

I've got a smoke here. Can you give me a cross, or are you still on the ground?

I'm up, but I don't see anything. What's your bearing?

Nine-three degrees, four-zero minutes, possibly in the southwest of twenty-three, thirty-two nine, west of the fifth.

Okay. Give me a sec and I'll get back to you.

This is the first time she has had a reason to speak to Gilmore directly, and she's all business. *Thanks. Clear to you. XMB four-five, this is XMA six-six-eight.*

Six-six-eight, this is Ron at dispatch. I caught that. How far out is it?

I'm guessing about twenty-five kilometres, but I might be off a bit. If Gilmore can give me a cross I can pin it down. Do you want me to pass a smoke message now, or should I wait?

No, don't wait. I'll take it now if you've got it.

I need a minute. I looked for a permit too, but I don't remember one out there, and the permanent log doesn't show anything.

There is a pause, and Percy knows that the duty officer is checking his own map. Barely a beat passes before he's back.

Could be some bear hunters got careless. What's it doing?

It's still pretty small, but it's growing. It's light grey, drifting a bit. I can't see the base, but it's definitely bigger than it was five minutes ago.

Okay. Keep an eye on it. Dispatch clear.

Six-six-eight.

Six-six-eight, this is six-four-nine.

Go ahead, Gilmore.

I don't know, Percy, I can't see anything. He speaks quickly. Everyone listening knows that if this fire is unattended, the winds are high enough to take it from a minor flare-up to one of major consequence in only a few hours.

Percy keys her mike. *Okay, Gilmore. Let me know if anything changes. Six-six-eight.*

The duty officer at headquarters cuts in. *Six-six-eight, this is dispatch.*

Dispatch, six-six-eight.

We're going to go with that location you gave Gilmore. Do you still have the smoke in sight?

Affirmative.

What's it doing now?

Percy holds the binoculars to her eyes with one hand, the mike to her mouth with the other. *It's flaring up a bit.*

What about the colour? Has it changed at all?

It might be a little darker, but pretty much the same.

What are your winds doing?

She tries to recall the wind speed she reported at afternoon weather, but she draws a blank. Seconds tick by. It's now that matters, not three hours ago. She sticks her head out a window to check the anemometer cups. They're spinning wildly. The weather vane points north. Treetops sway. It feels like an eternity since the duty officer asked about the wind. She knows that anxiety heightens this illusion, but she still feels a moment of panic. At last, she keys the mike. Perhaps twenty seconds have passed. *I'd say the wind is from the south at about three-zero kilometres.*

That's copied. Get me your smoke message and let me know if anything changes. We'll get someone out there right away. Dispatch clear.

Again there is no break before another tower calls. *XMA six-six-eight, this is XMC eight-four-five.*

This voice is unfamiliar—Percy can't put a name to the call sign. *Eight-four-five, this is six-six-eight.*

He is loud, slow, stammering, and his volume adds to her jumpiness. *I heard you call in. I think I see something to the southwest ... I'm not saying it's your smoke. I couldn't say for sure ... there's a ridge ... but you can check it out if you want. It might be a cloud, but it might be your smoke.*

As he speaks, Percy fills blanks on the smoke message, tries to place the voice. She looks at the map, where she has written the call signs of all the surrounding towers, even those she never hears. Eight-four-five is not listed. As soon as he breaks, she cuts in. *Which tower is this again, please?*

Six-six-eight, this is eight-four-five. This is Dave. Dave at Deer Lake. Deer Lake Tower.

Deer Lake Tower! Percy snorts. The guy's two hundred kilometres away—with normal reception, she wouldn't even hear him. She tries to sound cheerful. *Okay, Dave. I appreciate your help, but this smoke is pretty small yet. I don't think you'd be able to see it, actually. Thanks, anyway.*

Why is it that these guys always make themselves known when they're least wanted? She remembers someone cutting in on her last year as well. She sees three, four smokes a year, if she's lucky, and it's always then that some stranger chooses to help.

His voice is louder, more insistent. *This smoke I'm seeing is not small. My bearing is two-one-zero degrees and one-three minutes. No. That should be two-one-zero degrees and ... No. Stand by.*

Percy looks around exasperated. She doesn't have time for this.

Gilmore cuts in. *Six-six-eight, this is six-four-nine. I've got a bearing on your smoke.*

Go ahead, Gilmore.

My bearing on that is one-four-three degrees, one-five minutes. That'd put it about where you thought. Probably northeast of twenty-three, thirty-two nine.

Yes! she says aloud. Then, into the mike, *Great! Thanks Gilmore. Appreciate that. Dispatch, did you catch that cross?*

Affirmative. We got that. Are you ready with your smoke message?

That's affirmative. Stand by one, please.

Six-six-eight, this is eight-four-five.

Good God! Can't dispatch hear this guy? Somebody should tell him to get the hell off the radio. Percy's voice is brusque. *Eight-four-five, can I get you to hold off? I've got a smoke report to get in.*

I understand that, and this might be another smoke I see, but ...

Percy jiggles from one leg to the other, waiting for him to

continue his sentence. He could stammer all day long, but she can say nothing until he releases the key on his mike.

Get off the fucking radio, she yells out the window.

... well, anyway, it's kind of far to tell. But you got the luck today, that's for sure. Eight-four-five, clear.

Go away, Percy says. Then politely, into the mike, *Okay, eight-four-five. I guess so. Thanks for your help. Six-six-eight, clear.*

She turns to the map, grasps the string attached to the centre of the spot marked Weldon Lake Tower, and pulls it taut at 143 degrees, fifteen minutes, until it crosses the string that she ran out along her own bearing. Where they cross is the location of the fire. She double-checks the numbers and jots them on the smoke report, her first of the season.

The radio blares non-stop. Helicopter MCJ is only a few minutes south of the location. They have the smoke in sight and will fly over to check it out. That's luck. Percy waits for a break in radio traffic, then calls headquarters.

Dispatch, this is six-six-eight with my smoke report.

Go ahead, Percy.

Okay. To XMB four-five from Envy River Tower, today's date at this time. Number one is smoke number one. Number two is one-six-three-eight. Number three, nine-three degrees, four-zero minutes. Number four, small. Number five, light grey. Six, light column. Seven, drifting high ...

She runs through the required information: smoke number, time spotted, bearing, base visible or not, colour of smoke, size of column and whether it is drifting or rising straight up, approximate location, cross bearing, and from which tower the cross bearing was received. When she finishes, she watches through her binoculars and waits, her mind turning to Gilmore. He sounded friendly and helpful, called her by name; but has he read her message? Nothing in his voice suggested that he had, but then again, how would she know?

She keeps her binoculars focused on the smoke. Now that the helicopter has located the fire, she will relay messages from ground to air, if needed. Her adrenaline high subsides, and she feels a familiar vulnerability. Always there is this same letdown after a smoke, the excitement gone, and her role, so momentarily crucial, diminished once more.

Last year, she had three smokes, only one of them big enough to create any lasting excitement, and even then, her part was mostly over in an hour. Smoke from northern fires had drifted down and obscured visibility over the entire province, so she hadn't even seen the fire until it was huge—nearly ten hectares before she spotted it. After that, all hell broke loose. The fire was only twelve kilometres from her tower, so first she heard all the flak. Was she *certain* she had no visibility? Could she really see *zero* kilometres, or could she see one kilometre, maybe two? Maybe twelve? Even supposing she couldn't, couldn't she tell the difference in colour between the pinkish-brown smoke of the previous few days and these huge white pillars?

Of course she could; that's how she eventually spotted the damn thing. A few more days and it might have been licking into her own backyard, and the last thing she wanted was to be airlifted out while her tower burned to the ground, leaving her unemployed for the rest of the summer. Even now she gets heated up thinking about their questions.

Percy must also be careful to report smokes, not fires. Even if she can see flames leaping six feet high, she cannot call the blaze a fire until one of the rangers confirms that it is. But the big one last year was a fire all right, and an exciting one.

Approximately an hour after she reported it, the bombers arrived with their cargo of retardant. They flew over in formation, big hollow birds, dropping loads of sticky chemical at the head of the fire to stop its progress. When stopping the fire was not immediately possible, they worked to at least slow the burn. While the planes battled the head of the fire, bulldozers scraped day and night to clear the surrounding area and create fire breaks of bare dirt to contain the flames. Eventually, this strategy did stop the fire, if only because there were no strong back winds to help the flames jump over the breaks.

Meanwhile, two helicopters worked other hot spots, and after only one full day, the fire boss called a BH on the fire. It was no longer *out of control* but was *being held*. The bombers went home, and the two helicopters stayed, dipping buckets of water from a nearby lake to drop on the blaze. Percy entertained herself watching the choppers come and go.

It wasn't long before the fire was upgraded to *under control*. UC. One helicopter remained to dump the odd bucket of water and to transport people and equipment, but mostly attack crews used pumps and thousands of feet of hose to fight the fire from the ground. The firefighters set up camp within walking distance of the fire, and two crews lived there until the fire was extinguished.

Like her summers, theirs consist of long periods of routine punctuated by brief frenzies of panic. With one difference. Over the course of a summer, the crew members bond and forge face-to-face friendships.

The firefighters work hard, she knows, but they also crack jokes and look out for each other. All Percy can do is relay an occasional answer from a weak ground radio to someone at the ranger station asking questions.

So that was her biggest fire ever, and within ten days it was extinguished. The one she has spotted today won't last more than a day or two, at most.

Dispatch, this is MCJ.

The voice of the ranger speaking to headquarters from the helicopter breaks into her thoughts.

Go ahead, Jake.

Check us over the fire. Looks like we've got a stand of birch burning pretty fast. The good news is that we're nearly on top of a lake.

Have you had a chance to do an assessment? Do you know how big she is or what kind of men and equipment we're talking?

We're looking at about decimal zero-five hectares, but the wind's pushing things north. So long as the wind holds, looks like she'll burn right into the lake.

What's happening east west?

As long as the wind doesn't change, we'll be okay. There's not much fuel on either side, a cut-block and a thin stand of black spruce, so far as I can tell.

Do you have a bucket on board?

That's affirmative. We can start dropping water behind it and along the east-west perimeter, but we're going to need a squad, a couple of pumps, and about fifteen hundred feet of hose.

That's copied. I'll take your initial assessment report ASAP.

Affirmative. Stand by one.

Percy starts down the ladder, listening to the outside speaker as she descends. Now that they've found the smoke, the men will work well into the night. In fact, with daylight meaning little in their own smoky hell, they may work all night, if that's what is required to get the fire under control. If they need her, she will be here. She may cry between calls, may wrap her arms around herself and rock in place, may whimper like a baby, but no one will know.

Two

IN 1975, Percy is nine, and trailers in the small town of Oldrock still resemble long, rippled railway cars. They are not yet called mobile homes or prefabricated houses, but are simply trailers—sheets of corrugated metal riveted to long rectangular frames. *For People on the Go*, brochures of the time proclaim, although few of the people Percy knows go anywhere.

Her only friends, like her, live in Wes's Trailer Court, where thirty-some-odd trailers, aligned in double rows, share a plot of land with a public Laundromat. One scarred weeping birch grows near the entrance to the trailer court—a deceptive suggestion of what might, but does not, grow within—and provides a small patch of shade for adults and teens who lie belly down, as if they wish to protect what remains of their soft undersides. Children climb the branches and nearly everyone, adult or child, carves into the bark. Names, initials, and poorly inscribed symbols invite more. You too, they seem to say, can contribute to the history of your neighbourhood.

On the day that Percy Turner meets Marlea Dunn, Percy is perched on the hitch of her parents' trailer, observing the tractor truck as it backs the Dunns' trailer into the stall next door. A girl about her own age edges up to her.

Hi, she says, and peers at Percy from a friendly, heart-shaped face. I'm Marlea Dunn and I'm nine years old. My eyes are different colours. Only one person in a thousand has eyes like that, and my dad says it means I'm going to be famous. Yours are yellow.

Marlea's eyes are indeed different colours—one green, one brown—and a bit watery, like those of a happy, curious puppy.

Mine are amber, Percy says. Some people have amber eyes. She squints at Marlea and waits to be challenged. When Marlea merely nods and smiles in an interested way, Percy points to her mouth. I can fold my tongue in half.

She demonstrates by flipping the front half of her tongue toward the back of her mouth. With her tongue still folded, she forces the veiny underside past her lips until she sees that the raw ugliness of her ability impresses Marlea.

Try it, she says.

But Marlea can't hold the fold without clamping it between her front teeth. I bet there aren't many kids who can do that, she says.

Percy's shoulders relax. I know there aren't. D'you want to see my rocks?

She pulls a tin plate out from under the step and shows Marlea the pebbles and bits of coloured glass she has collected, agates from down by the river and black ones flecked with silver. Fool's gold, she says, and this green one looks like malachite when it's wet, but it's not. We don't have malachite here.

Later, the girls fill a Roger's syrup can with water and soak the flowers in Percy's yard. The tiny lawn contains mostly coarse quack grass and chickweed. Her mother doesn't waste money on expensive, exotic plants, but every spring she digs up the same small, fenced semicircle of earth around the trailer hitch and plants pansies and geraniums. The pansies wilt under the blood-red flowers and coarse stalks of her mother's geraniums, but Percy tends them daily, stroking their petals and encouraging them to survive.

Look how skinny their stems are, she says to Marlea,

who, in her thin and happy way, reminds Percy of a pale pansy. Next to the pansies, the geraniums look like weeds.

The pansies are kind of frail, Marlea says. At least the geraniums take care of themselves.

Percy introduces Marlea to her older brother, Bobby, and to Annette, who lives a couple of rows over and is only eight. Until Percy meets Marlea, Annette is her best friend. Now Annette stands before them scratching pieces of dead skin from her scalp. She examines a piece the size of her fingernail, then pops it into her mouth while Percy and Marlea watch.

She has psoriasis, Percy whispers to Marlea, by way of an apology. We don't have to play with her if you don't want to. Her happiness at being chosen by Marlea allows her to ignore a momentary twinge of shame.

After that, Marlea and Percy spend all of their time together, only calling on Annette when they need three people to skip long-rope or to play elastics. Even then, they aren't nice about needing her.

One, two, three, pickin' at your head. Four, five, six, findin' somethin' dead, Percy and Marlea sing as they jump.

When Annette can no longer stand their taunts, she grabs her end of the plastic rope and swings it into the air, flailing her arms until the hard handle connects with Percy's back, makes red welts on Marlea's bare legs.

My mom says you're evil, she shouts at Percy. Even your own mom thinks so. Everyone knows.

Percy lunges at her and throws her to the ground. With a fistful of Annette's hair in her hand, she demands an apology. But Marlea is screaming and pulling on Percy.

She'll tell and you'll be in even more trouble. Marlea wipes her nose on her hand and whimpers. Percy, please. Stop.

Percy gives Annette's hair a final yank and gets to her feet, relieved in part that Marlea has given her a way out. You watch your mouth, she says. I could get you any time I want.

Annette is crying too. I meant it, she says. You're evil.

Marlea wipes her nose again and pulls Percy away. C'mon. Your mom will kill you.

I'll kill *her*, Percy says, pointing at Annette. But she knows she can't afford more trouble.

Only four days ago she was caught snooping through her mother's purse, looking for change. Within minutes, she lay bare-bottomed over the end of her bed. Marlea said she could hear them next door, every second or third syllable of Percy's mother's words accompanied by the force of leather on bare flesh. Don't you EVER do THAT aGAIN.

When Percy finally gave in and cried, her mother shut the door on her so she could think about the consequences of disrespect. A few moments later, she returned with a mirror. Look, she said. Look at that ugly face. That's what you look like when you cry.

Now, whenever Percy cries, she covers her face so no one will have to witness how ugly she is.

PERCY earns a crafts badge in Pioneer Girls by constructing a miniature of her family's trailer from a Velveeta cheese box: one-and-a-half inches at the front for the kitchen, two-and-a-half inches for the living room, then three bedrooms and a bathroom narrowed by the width of a hall. She wraps the whole thing in pleated tinfoil and paints it white. Then, as much to please her mother as to maintain the integrity of her model, she licks red and purple stars and pastes them on the front. They are disproportionate, but like the real flowers they add colour to the drab exterior.

She tries to reconstruct her family's furniture as well, but when she shows the first miniature to her mother—a red velvet couch made from covered cardboard, complete with small tears in the cushions—Mrs. Turner is not amused. The good Lord provided these things, she says, her tone implying that Percy should be smart enough to know better, and I'm happy to have them.

Her mother is right, of course, and Percy's stomach clenches. She hunches forward, her shoulder blades rising like ready bird wings. She drops the tiny couch to the floor and lowers her eyes. She didn't mean to poke fun.

Mrs. Turner sets her paper aside. The headline on the front page stands out in bold black: Woman Loses 150 Pounds Following the Jesus Diet. She folds the paper in half, then gestures at Percy's miniature, the edge gone out of her voice. Pick that up. Let me see it again.

Mrs. Turner's fingers are mottled red, rough and sore-looking as she extends her hand, and tiny blisters mark burns from a hot iron.

Percy squats to retrieve the miniature. She doesn't look at her mother, just crumples the piece and jams it into her pocket before her mother can see. It's old, she says. I only meant it to be old.

USUALLY, Percy tries to stay out of her parents' way, but once in a while her father loops an arm over her shoulder and points to his cheek, saying, Put one here, Squeak.

When he says that, Percy kisses his cheek and rests her face against his, breathing in the oily, sweaty odour of town labour—dust and salt and tar. She wishes her father called her Squeak more often, but too soon, as if she might settle in and get comfortable in a way he cannot tolerate, he pulls back. He gives her shoulder a quick squeeze and says, You're a good kid, Priscilla, a good kid.

Usually, her mother steps in then, pulls her eyebrows together and flashes her eyes at Percy. He's in a good mood, her face warns. Don't spoil it. So Percy will move aside and watch her mother's face relax. Mrs. Turner's smile is fleeting but sincere when she pats Percy on the arm, or pets her hair, as if she too would like to hug her daughter.

Percy is relieved to see her mother soften some. Most days, she seems wound tight, angry about something Percy can never understand and is afraid to question.

During the day, her mother stands in the bedroom ironing in silence. The radio jangles her nerves, she says, so there is nothing but her thoughts for company. It must be her thoughts, Percy thinks, that make her so tight and angry. Or perhaps she dislikes the way her eerie silence is shattered when Percy slams the door on her way in after school, or the way the trailer creaks and moans as Percy moves down the hall to the kitchen. There, even the sound of the fan in the refrigerator is deafening as Percy searches for a snack that her mother won't miss.

Have a piece of bread, Mrs. Turner says whenever she hears the refrigerator door open. It's almost time for supper.

Percy fails to understand how she can pass the entire length of the trailer, from bathroom to kitchen, without seeing her mother along the way, and then, poof, there she is behind Percy at the refrigerator, adding, And wash up and set the table while you're here, please.

Next door, the Dunns' radio customarily blares on the kitchen counter while TV programs come and go in the living room. Percy often sees Mrs. Dunn move up and down the length of the trailer, swaying to music as she folds a towel or pauses in front of the TV on her way past.

Look at this, she often says. Can you believe it?

On the TV screen might be a cartoon, the news, *Merv Griffin*, or *The Brady Bunch*. Mrs. Dunn doesn't discriminate between television programs—almost every show has something to offer if you're open to it, Percy has heard her say.

None of this impresses Percy's parents, and it is her father who most often rants about the neighbours, particularly about that damn godawful eyesore staring him in the face every time he looks out the window. Mrs. Turner usually nods and shushes him. Don't swear, she'll say, glancing at Percy, who has heard language much worse at school and occasionally from her mother as well.

Just look at it, her father says. I don't give a good goddamn if the guy's fool enough to spend his money on a piece of rattletrap shit, but does he have to park it right outside my goddamn window? Look at that. He points out the window to the old blue bus parked and peeling beside the Dunns' trailer. Look at that damn ugly thing, why don't you? Useless. Damned useless how it sits there all year.

But every Friday evening, from grade six onward, Marlea

and Percy lock themselves in the bus. The routine is always the same—Percy scrabbles out of pants and T-shirt and rummages in an I G A bag for the limp pyjamas she totes. She tugs them on, then she hoists herself onto the top bunk, where she rests her chin on the edge of the mattress and watches as Marlea undresses for bed. Marlea doesn't object to Percy's gaping at her, but simply carries on as if she were doing any old thing. She turns her T-shirt right side out and hangs it on a nail, then squares into proper posture and raises both hands behind her back to undo the hooks of her bra. Sometimes Percy's hands perspire as she watches, and she rubs them on her pyjamas; other times she is oblivious to anything but the white lace of Marlea's bra stretching taut before it relaxes against her chest.

Percy doesn't understand why Marlea's bra remains bright white while her own panties and undershirts turn grey so quickly, but that is Marlea, as inexplicable to Percy as her own heart sucking against her ribs while she watches. The bra never falls until Marlea hunches her shoulders and shrugs loose, but when she does, her breasts—her entire upper body—looks supple and polished. Her flesh stretches smooth and elastic like Percy's, is inscribed with tan lines similar to Percy's, yet Marlea's body has become womanly alone.

WHEN they are both thirteen, Marlea and Percy sit across from one another on the bottom bunk of the bus. In the heat, they have stripped to their panties, even their bras discarded. Marlea leans against the wall at the head of the bed; Percy leans against the one at the foot. The stiff sleeping bag on which they sit spread-legged rustles with every movement, and from between Percy's legs wafts the wet-pillow odour of damp nylon undies—three for $1.99 at Robinson's department store. After one wash they lose all body and become nearly transparent so that, from the back, the crack in Percy's butt shows as a shadowy arc. Her pubic hairs have grown in four or five at a time, not curly but kinky-straight, beginning with a few strands between her legs, then inching upward toward her belly—and they too are clearly visible through the limp nylon. Visible enough that Susan Martin notices and comments on the quality of Percy's underwear as she changes after gym class.

That's an interesting idea, Susan says. Panties made from plastic wrap.

Percy flushes. Yeah, I keep a spare pair wrapped around my sandwich.

She looks to Marlea for help, but Marlea has become suddenly busy in her locker. A chorus of girls exchange glances and titter while Percy strips and stands under the shower. She hates Susan Martin. She hates her straight, pointy nose, hates her long polished fingernails, even hates her dull metallic braces because although food sticks in them now, Percy knows that someday Susan will have perfectly white, corn kernel teeth, while her own will

36

remain irregular. Percy hates Susan's unlimited supply of soft, fashionable clothing, her pretty, lacy underwear, and she especially hates that everything she resents about Susan makes her popular, while Percy sits at her desk too afraid to raise her hand because, if she does, all anyone will see are the wet patches under her arms, the patches in stark contrast with the drier fabric of her cheap, but well-ironed, blouse. Percy will not allow Susan Martin to see her cry.

The next week, rather than change in front of the other girls, Percy avoids them all, even Marlea, by arriving early. She sits in a toilet cubicle made unpleasant by the fumes of a commercial deodorizer caged high on the wall. Inside the locked grid a new green block has begun to dissolve. So new that the corners are not yet rounded, the deodorizer perspires tiny drops of chemical sweat. Percy cups her hands over her nose and mouth, imagines green drops in the air, green drops accumulating on her nose hairs as she breathes, stalactites growing from her tonsils, dripping green down her throat. She considers the necessity of the lock that keeps the smelly chunk dissolving on the wall. Who, she wonders, would even consider stealing a congealed lump of air freshener?

Breathing in and out through her fingers, she waits for her classmates to change into their gym shorts, listens to their chatter, listens for Marlea, but hears, above the voices of the other girls, Susan Martin.

Where's Percy today? Stocking up on sandwich wrap?

Percy holds her breath, waits for the response. Some of the girls laugh, then Susan speaks again. You don't really like her, do you?

There is a pause, then Marlea answers, her voice conciliatory and hesitant. Yeah. I don't know …

Her mom's crazy, you know. A religious nutcake. Susan

sounds smug and self-important with the weight of her knowledge.

They're bad, says a quiet voice Percy can't place. My mom says they have no morals. She told me to stay away from her.

What? Whose mom told her to stay away? Percy waits until she can no longer hear the girls, then she checks in each toilet stall to be certain she is alone. Her stomach burns with unspoken rage at Marlea's betrayal. And Susan is a fat-headed jerk.

In the change area, she has no trouble recognizing the neat pile of clothing that can only belong to Susan Martin, and quickly, before anyone returns from the gym, she lifts the smart red slacks from the pile and shakes them out. Because she will never own a pair so new and expensive, Percy sneers at the cuffs on the bottom. Church pants. As she is never allowed to wear anything but a dress to church, the thought only rankles her further.

She bunches the red crotch into a small puff of fabric and returns to a toilet cubicle. Her heart thumps with nastiness as she pulls down her second-hand stretch pants. When she finishes what she has come to do, she will dry the Sunday slacks under the hand-blower, and that bitch Susan Martin can wonder all day why she smells of urine. Better yet, everyone else can wonder. Percy relishes the thought of whispers in the hall, of odd looks and sniggering girls.

Except, for no reason she understands, the whole plan seems suddenly stupid and pointless. Although she had wanted to get even with Susan, it is Marlea's words that are hurting her now, and she doesn't dare get even. *I don't know,* Marlea said, and Percy knows her options. She can confront Marlea—yell at her or cry like a two-year-old—which might result in Marlea's becoming another of

Susan's cliquish admirers, or she can silently forgive her, pretending she has heard nothing. If there are other choices, they don't occur to her.

Percy can't swallow past the lump in her throat, her head aches, and the predictable burning in her stomach jabs like a hot nail. Soon it will be a knife, but she will not cry. Instead, she pees a steady stream into the toilet and pulls her pants up. The thought of fighting with Marlea over Susan Martin seems just as stupid and pointless as everything else. She adjusts her sweater, then folds Susan's slacks along their expensive crease and puts them back where she found them.

On the bunk with Marlea, Percy doesn't worry about the transparency of her panties. Her legs are just long enough so that she can press the soles of Marlea's feet comfortably as she sits opposite her on the bunk. Every few seconds, Marlea scrunches Percy's toes and Percy either scrunches back or presses her heels tight against Marlea's. All ten toenails stand out like shiny pink candies. Rose Petal Enamel states the tiny label on the bottom of the bottle, and Percy likes how heavy and thick the enamel feels when her toes click against the walls of the bus.

Next to the plastic brightness of their toenails, the girls' skin is tanned and scuffed. Percy watches as Marlea's breasts lift on an intake of air and fall back on each long exhalation. She looks at her own chest and strokes the swelling around her nipples. Where Marlea's breasts are nicely rounded, hers scarcely protrude.

Feel this, Percy says. Did yours get a hard lump when they started to grow?

Marlea strains forward to reach Percy's nipple. She manipulates it with one finger. Does it hurt?

Only if I bump them.

I remember that. If you bump them too hard they get crushed and don't grow.

Percy nearly chokes. She has been sucking on a pebble—a small, flat oval she found in the river and stores in her mouth. If she sets it aside while she eats or sleeps, the beautiful emerald colour transforms into mere gravel as it dries. She coughs and pulls the stone from her mouth.

She recalls the rough concrete walls of the school stairwell and hears the teacher's raised voice: Careful, now. Walk, don't run. And *no pushing*, Robert.

One hundred and twenty students from the third floor pushing and shoving as they try to escape the ear-aching clamour of an unexpected fire alarm. Percy remembers the searing pain of Patsy's elbow connecting with her right breast as they reach the second-floor landing, the track-hardened back of a grade nine boy she slams into at the bottom.

Are mine broken? She stares wide-eyed at Marlea, waits for a verdict.

Marlea forms four fingers into a pliant pad and gently rotates each of Percy's nipples. Hot fingerprints remain on one breast when she moves to the other. No, she says, having decided at last, but you've got to be careful.

Percy nods. She pops the pebble back into her mouth and rests against the wall while Marlea continues her examination. When Percy's nipples pucker, Marlea withdraws for a moment, then settles only her index finger on the tip of one breast. The heat from her finger flattens the pucker into a round, puffy sphere, and with ever-so-soft strokes, she draws tentative spokes outward from the centre of Percy's aureola. Percy feels as if she is breathing through a hot, wet cloth; the bus is suddenly too quiet for the noise of her shallow, panting breath. Tiny rivulets escape her armpits.

Let me feel yours, she says.

As gingerly as Marlea touched hers, Percy pushes on one nipple. It springs back as soon as she stops applying pressure. Marlea's nipples are bigger than her own, and they shine a faint pink that barely contrasts with the surrounding skin. Percy slides her palm under Marlea's breast and lifts the entire soft weight. Marlea's nipple shrinks to the size of a pale raspberry, and once again, Percy gasps for air, but no oxygen reaches her lungs. She will die right here, gasping for breath, unless she removes her hand from Marlea's breast.

Her diaphragm moves in and out to a wild, frightened beat; her lungs refuse to cooperate. She pulls her hand back and draws her knees against her chest. She opens her mouth, wants to say: Let's go make footprints in the dust. Instead, she gags on her sucking stone.

As for the change-room talk about her family's morals, Percy knows those girls haven't a clue. Her mother is always talking about morality, and every Sunday, regardless of the weather, Mrs. Turner dons her good clothes and walks to the Church of the Nazarene.

In the spring and summer, she wears a powder blue suit or a calf-length skirt with a sweater set. In the fall and winter she wears black shoes instead of white, and the dress is a one-piece knit. Not one of the outfits is fashionable, and all are spicy with the scent of too many wearings, but like the good china set only on holidays, they are distinguished by the infrequency of their use.

Sometimes Uncle George calls to say he is going that way anyway and will give Percy's mother a lift to church if she'd like. He's not really an uncle, just a friend who works for the town, like Percy's father. He drives one of the town trucks, hauling dirt and gravel in the summer and sand in the winter. Percy's father often works alongside him, operating the only grader.

Uncle George lives in the row of trailers directly behind the Turners, and if Percy is attentive, she can almost always hear him start the engine of his Chevy Impala. Sometimes, when Percy's mother is in the middle of doing something else, she will lift her head and smile at Percy. There's George, she'll say, and sure enough, if Percy listens, she will hear the distinctive rumble of Uncle George's muffler. Then she and her mom will both follow the deep reverberations until the sound either stops in front of their own trailer or fades away as he turns out onto the highway that runs past the trailer court and straight through Oldrock.

If Uncle George arrives a bit early, he sits on the steps with Percy's father, the two of them drinking beer while they wait for Percy's mother to say she's ready. Uncle George doesn't have a wife or any children of his own, so he's extra friendly to Percy and Bobby. In summer he sometimes takes them for ice cream or gives them each five dollars and drops them at the Lux for a Saturday matinee.

Take your time, he says, I'll keep your mom off your back. Then he winks conspiratorially and grins, running his hand over his shiny bald scalp as if he has forgotten there is no longer any hair to push back.

Even with his short, wide nose and only a fringe of hair connecting his ears, Percy secretly thinks he is far handsomer than her father, and she loves the way his skin crinkles like happy stars at the ends of his eyes. In particular, she looks forward to the Sunday mornings when Uncle George gives her mother a ride, partly because he is fun and easy to have around, but mostly because whenever she has a lift, Mrs. Turner doesn't require that Bobby and Percy accompany her to church. Instead, she allows them to remain at home to read comic books or watch television with their father, who says it's no skin off his nose if she wants to be married to Christ, just so long as she remembers who puts food on the table and tends to her duties the way she ought to.

When he talks like that, Mrs. Turner frowns and mutters about the ways of the devil and how even the most faithful of the Lord's servants are led astray. The devil lives in this house, she says, and I don't see you trying to do anything about it.

The devil lives where he gets noticed, seems to me, and I

ain't noticing, so you go to church if you like, but you remember what I say. And you keep them people away from me. I've had more than enough of them. Percy's father looks meaningfully at her mother, then at Uncle George, and that is where the conversation ends.

If Uncle George responds to this kind of talk at all, it is usually with a joke or some smart retort, but Percy can tell that her father makes him feel uncomfortable when he looks at him like that, because before Uncle George reacts, he inevitably tips his empty beer bottle back as if there were still something in it, or notices a spot on his boot that needs a good spit-and-finger polish—little distractions Percy might try if one of her parents were aiming long spiked glances her way.

Shortly after noon, on these Sundays, Uncle George's car comes rumbling to a stop in front of the trailer again, and Mrs. Turner's face shines. Uncle George never comes in for lunch, just drops her off special delivery before going on his way.

Just as well he doesn't come in, says Mr. Turner. He never brings his own damn beer anyway. Just sucks mine back like water. This is said without malice, just offered up as a fact for anyone who cares to listen.

But Mrs. Turner pointedly ignores his remarks and merely sneaks surreptitious glances at her reflection in the kitchen window, singing hymns under her breath as she pulls smooth white bread from a bag. She often stacks seven or eight slices on a bread plate, a small tower only she and Percy's father will eat, and then dinner—or *lunch*, as Marlea's parents call it—is ready.

All right, everybody, Mrs. Turner says then. Come and get it.

With less weariness than usual, she serves the stew or

whatever else she set to simmer before she left in the morning. Then she bows her head.

Thank you, Lord, for this food, she always begins, saying the grace herself, in genuinely thankful tones. All that is required of everyone else is that they keep their eyes closed and their mouths shut.

THERE is a photo of her mother that Percy likes to look at. It rests on a shelf in the living room, and shows her mother sitting on a bench by the lake. She looks young, although she was nearly forty when it was taken. They hadn't gone to the lake often, and on that day Percy had asked if Marlea could accompany them. But no, she couldn't. There was only room for herself and Bobby, for her parents, and for Uncle George.

Some of the other photographs from this roll show Percy off by herself pouting, ignoring family and camera as best she could, but in the photo she likes, Uncle George has turned to face Percy's mother on the bench. Neither of them looks at the camera, or the lake, but only at each other, hair blowing off their faces, eyes squinting against the sun. Her father must have taken the photo, and she often wonders if he noticed the softness in her mother's face that day. Perhaps that's why he took the picture in the first place.

In any event, this is the only photo in which Percy sees some resemblance between her mother and herself. It isn't that they look much alike—Percy has wild autumn-red hair, while her mother's is smooth and brown. Her nose is short and wide, where her mother's is long. Not even the shapes of their faces are similar, as her mother's face is much rounder and doesn't have the same square jaw that Percy has. Still, there is something in her mother's expression that seems familiar. Percy recognizes a certain surrender of self-consciousness in her mother that has been captured in photos of herself with Marlea. Her mother sits erect, neither tired and resigned, nor strained and impatient, only ready, as if she anticipates something original and unexpected, as if that is the reason her mouth has abandoned its straight line, has left her lips softly hopeful. Percy recognizes the eagerness she often feels when she is with Marlea, the sense that something good could happen at any minute, and must.

Yet what happens to Uncle George, only a month or two later, surprises them all.

He's just up and gone, Percy's mother says. His precious car, his trailer and all. He's up and left. She looks as if she can't believe this impossibility. After all, she only stepped outside to check the box for mail, the same as every other day. When she looked up, she saw that ugly empty gap, like a missing tooth, where Uncle George's trailer should have been.

Who's gone? says Percy's father. He shuffles outside to look for himself. When he returns, he looks as surprised and disoriented as his wife, even more so because of the baffled anger they can all see rising from the base of his neck, colouring his face, until he stands there in the middle of the living room looking from his wife to his children and back again, as if he is ready to find either one or all of them responsible for every unfavourable thing that has ever happened to him. No one approaches him, not even Bobby, until finally he sinks down on the edge of the couch and shakes his head. Well, don't that just beat all, he says. Don't that just beat all.

Mrs. Turner doesn't even look at her husband then; she just walks over to Bobby and Percy, and like some syrupy television mom, she hugs each of them stiffly, the way she does on their birthdays. You go on now, she says. Go on and get to school before you're late.

All day, time drags for Percy. She doesn't know why Uncle George has left without saying goodbye, but she knows she'll miss him. At four o'clock, she and Bobby rush home, eager to see what has transpired in their absence. Either their father has quit work early, or he didn't go in at all. Whichever it is, he and their mother are clearly arguing.

It sure as hell couldn't have been any harder on him all these years than it's been on me, Mr. Turner is practically shouting as they enter. And even if it was, you don't just up and disappear without a goddamn trace! We all agreed from the beginning how it'd be. I thought we were making the best of it—

Walter, that's enough! Their mother, who has been sagging in a chair, rises to her feet. The way she holds her lips tightly together, entire paragraphs might be compressed behind her teeth, thin lines of angry words barely waiting their turn.

For all of Mrs. Turner's snapping at Percy and Bobby, Percy has never heard her dare to order their father about. She steps back, not knowing how to prepare for what may happen next. But Mr. Turner just stares at his wife for a long, extended moment. Maybe he really sees her clearly, because now that she has made her stand, she slumps against the wall, all limp acquiescence again, as if it is all she can do to stay upright. Her face is pale, and her eyes, like her body, have surrendered.

Their father stands looking, and while he looks, his eyes fill with tears. Finally, he crosses to where their mother leans against the wall, and lowering his head to her shoulder, he weeps—huge, horrid, honking sobs that leave Percy and Bobby white-faced and speechless. Mouths gaping, they stare at their father's wet features pushed into their mother's neck. They watch until she puts her hand on the back of his head and presses her own eyes, dry and squeezed shut, into his hair.

No, no, no, she moans, shaking her head over and over.

When Percy looks past her parents, she sees her reflection in the living room window, sees her whole family reflected like mannequins, no one moving, only her mother's head shaking back and forth.

C'mon, Bobby whispers. Let's get out of here.

Percy can feel his fingers tugging on her shirt, can hear him panting quietly behind her. When she turns to look at him, she sees her own confusion and fear mirrored on him, and something else—anger or impatience or even disgust.

Percy puts her hand over her mouth and follows him outside and down the road until they are behind the Laundromat. She slides her spine down the cool, solid concrete blocks, and comes to rest with her knees pulled close to her chest.

Bobby slides down beside her, then swings out at the empty air. Dad shoulda popped him in the mouth while he had a chance. He's got it coming, if you ask me.

Percy looks at Bobby swinging his fists in the air and feels an unreasonable urge to laugh. And to cry. She stares at her brother. But why? she says. Why would Dad want to do something like that?

Bobby shrugs. Cuz he's a prick. He's just a prick, that's all, and he's better off gone. Things'll get better now. You'll see.

AFTER Uncle George disappears, which is how people refer to his leaving, Mrs. Turner works even more hours than usual. Everything does not get better, as Bobby promised, only quieter, with no Uncle George to break the monotony.

Mrs. Turner advertises her services on bulletin boards at both the IGA grocery store and at the United Church, and she takes in ironing at seventy-five cents an item. On an average week, she makes about ninety dollars, more if the weather is particularly warm. Years ago, she did laundry as well, but what with her wringer always breaking, and the cost of soap, and the town charging more for water all the time, she has foregone laundry and limits herself to ironing.

She is open from eight to eleven in the morning, when her customers pick up and pay. The rest of the time, they slide bags or baskets of clothing through a chute into the front porch, and as often as not, every door, cupboard, and hook in her bedroom and down the hall is hung with the crisp apparel of strangers. She has a closet in the front porch too, where she hangs labelled sets of clothing every evening, and a shelf for folded items, but during the day she rarely stops for anything.

Of course she doesn't *like* the work, she tells Percy, but at least she sets her own hours and can dress as she pleases, in a loose housedress and comfortable slippers.

If I worked downtown, she says, I'd have to dress the part, and wear stockings, and buy special shoes, and how much would I bring home after all that? This way, I'm my own boss, and I'm doing something everybody hates, so they're happy to bring their business to me. You work in a shop and your customers think they're doing you a favour just coming in the door.

Mrs. Turner keeps a scribbler in the kitchen drawer, where she notes who owes what, and she has never had an argument.

Percy doesn't have to help with the ironing, but she has been babysitting since she was thirteen, and she is expected to continue. When she wants to stop after not even two years of experience, her mother acts as if she can't believe any daughter of hers could be so stupid.

Percy has been buying her own clothes since she began babysitting, and most of her school supplies as well, all from the money she earns. If it weren't for the Millers, she wouldn't have made enough money to buy diddly-squat, according to her mother.

All of this is true, Percy knows, but aside from quitting altogether, she can't think of any other way to avoid her growing attraction to Mr. Miller, an attraction she is certain is mutual. He often winks at her, and more than once she has caught him looking when he thinks she's unaware. Still, he's married to Mrs. Miller, and Percy keeps remembering something Uncle George said—you can let trouble find you, or you can walk away, but once trouble finds you, you're sunk. Even if you think you're not, he cautioned, you are. Instinctively, Percy knows Mr. Miller is someone she should walk away from.

Still, babysitting for the Millers is better than babysitting anywhere else. They leave her mixed nuts and Pepsi, sometimes even pizza, instead of popcorn and Kool-Aid like most people, and they always pay extra.

Mr. Miller sells farm equipment, and they own the only double-wide trailer in Wes's Trailer Court. Unlike anyone else, they rent two stalls in the back row—lots, they call them. The wooden wishing well is something Mrs. Miller made herself, and it is set off nicely by brick walkways and plenty of low-lying shrubs. Percy hopes she will live in just such a place when she grows up, so she notices everything and often wishes these luxuries were already hers.

The Millers' son, Derek, is only three months old when Percy first babysits him, and he is seldom awake when she arrives. Every half-hour or so, she peeks in his room and listens for the soft grunting noises she has learned to associate with peaceful sleep. His room is much warmer than the rest of the trailer and humid with baby breath, so although there is not a plant in sight, the room reminds Percy of an atrium she once visited on a school field trip, a warm, quiet place filled with the scent of moist earth. The atrium, and its utter serenity, moved her so deeply that she kept a handful of stolen dirt moistened in a jar for a whole year after the outing. Every day, she'd lift the lid and inhale deeply, trying to relive that one visit. She does the same in Derek's room, just stands there breathing, experiencing a sense of calm she never feels at home.

These days he rarely cries, and when she strokes his head with gentle fingers, or brushes her index finger down the side of his cheek, he smiles and babbles and eventually nods off to sleep. She often sits in the rocking chair watching him sleep, breathing in Derek's warm-milk odour and touching his fuzzy-soft sleepers to her own cheek.

In the master bedroom, Mrs. Miller has a vanity table built into a corner, and when Percy sits on a stool in front of the mirror, she likes to imagine Mr. Miller's freshly shaved face bending to kiss her own forehead as she completes her makeup.

You look lovely tonight, she imagines him saying, and

when she closes her eyes and concentrates very hard, she conjures his voice out of the air.

Tonight, as she has done a dozen other times, she takes the little blue stopper from a bottle of Evening in Paris perfume and passes the vial under her nose. She angles her head and stares off into a corner of the room, as if she can't decide whether the scent suits her mood or not. Deciding no, after all, she returns the bottle to the centre of the doily.

She clips pink pearl earrings onto her earlobes, and without guilt, she begins her examination of each item in the vanity table's four shallow drawers. In the top drawer, a flat silver-coloured box holds brooches, beads, and bracelets— bright jewelled things that don't tangle easily. Her favourite is a heavy cameo strung on a velvet ribbon rather than a chain. Percy holds this to her throat and fashions an image of herself from late-night movies, a young woman in a long low-cut gown, hooped wide at the hem so that it sways seductively as she walks. And boots. She needs button-up boots with a dress like that.

Percy abandons the other drawers for the closet. She has never checked the Millers' closet for shoes, although she has separated clothes crammed tightly together and has fingered Mr. Miller's shirts, bringing the fabric to her nose in search of that new male odour so different from the one worn into her father's wardrobe of sweaters and old work shirts. Mr. Miller's clothes smell like cologne and laundry, never like dust or oil.

Mrs. Miller must not have many shoes, Percy concludes, because she finds only one pair of navy pumps and some moccasins with trampled heels. There are no boots, except for a short plain pair so large that they must belong to Mr. Miller. The footwear is not lined up neatly, but is jumbled

Pearl Luke

together with winter gloves and stray hangers. Off to the side is a short stack of magazines.

Percy checks the magazines for anything of interest. *True Detective*, she finds, *True Romance*, *Redbook*, and one with no cover at all. She slides *Redbook* and *True Detective* back into the stack, but flips through *True Romance*. There are several pictures of women crying, and even those who aren't crying look sorrowful in such grainy black-and-white photos. Still, one story catches her eye. It is titled *I Caught My Husband With My Twin Sister*. The photo shows both twins dressed alike. Their clothes are torn, exposing their breasts and buttocks. Definitely worth a look, Percy thinks. She folds the magazine under her arm, for later, and turns the pages of the one with no cover.

This magazine is in black and white as well, and at first Percy thinks it is another *True Romance*, but she soon notices that the women are naked, except for black boxes that cover their eyes. Some of the men are naked too, but black boxes cover both their eyes and their private parts. Percy doesn't care. It is the women who interest her, most of them touching other women, hands on breasts or aiming pointy tongues at other pointy tongues. She throws the *True Romance* back in the closet and slides over to the wall to support her back.

An urgent pulse is making itself known between her legs, is rippling up into the muscles of her stomach, and she hears the same pulse in her ears, as if she has gone deaf from looking, instead of blind, as she feels she ought to. Some of the women on these pages are crying too, for good reason, blindfolded and bound, reaching out helplessly. Percy turns the pages quickly, stopping when she sees two girls her own age holding each other, gently it appears, smiling shyly as if oblivious to the camera recording them. Both girls have long straight blonde hair, and they kneel facing each other. The girl on the right has her hand under the other girl's breast, perhaps lifting it, feeling its weight just as Percy felt the weight of Marlea's breast that day in the bus.

Wait until Marlea hears about this! This is even better than the time she heard her parents fucking. Not that their fucking was such a big deal in the thin-walled trailer—the surprising bit was her father saying Mommy, Mommy, Mommy, over and over as the bed wheezed to a regular rhythm.

When she is sure she has looked at every page, Percy wipes her hands on her thighs and hides the magazine in the back of the closet, behind a box that looks permanently stashed. Maybe no one will find it. Maybe it will be there the next time she babysits.

Derek is soundly asleep, so she rubs his back and turns his head to one side the way Mrs. Miller has taught her. Then she settles on the kitchen linoleum with the telephone receiver securely wedged between her cheek and her shoulder.

Boy, do I have news for you, she says, as soon as Marlea answers. She waits an extra beat to build Marlea's curiosity, but she can't hold back for another second. Mrs. Miller's got a whole pile of dirty magazines in her closet. What do you think of that?

As best she can, Percy recounts the contents of the two magazines she looked at, blending details, stretching the truth where it will make the story stronger. Don't you think that's weird? That she has pictures of women?

Maybe they're Mr. Miller's.

This stops Percy for a moment. There was that *True Detective*, but she shakes her head. I don't think so. I never see Mr. Miller reading, just her.

She might be a lezzie.

Mrs. *Miller* might be a lezzie? Percy can tell by the way Marlea says the word *lezzie* that being one is not good. I don't know what that is.

A lesbian. A woman who does … you know … stuff … with other women. You know, who fools around with them.

This is the most amazing thing Percy has ever heard. There are women who fool around with each other, for real? Maybe even touch each other the way the women in the magazine were touching? Ever since that time in the bus, Percy has been obsessed with breasts. Smooth round plastic breasts on mannequins, vague covered breasts in catalogues, or uncovered as on the sculpture at the library, and the real live breasts of any woman bending over her, soft handfuls of flesh falling forward in their blouses. She would give anything to feel the soft heaviness of Marlea's breasts in her palms again.

No way, she says, in reference to Pamela Miller, but in part to her own desire for Marlea, which she knows has to be wrong. She's never heard of any other girls wanting to kiss or touch anyone but boys. Until now, that is, and she aches between her legs at the mere thought of these lesbian women.

But how, Percy asks, can Mrs. Miller be a lesbian if she is married and has a child? She doesn't seem like a lesbian to me. I like her.

Me too, so long as she doesn't try anything.

What do you mean, try anything? You think she'd be interested in us? Despite herself, a note of hope slides into Percy's voice.

By the time the Millers arrive home, Percy is asleep on their couch. The TV emits a low hum, and the multi-coloured stripes of the test pattern light the living room.

Percy.

Mrs. Miller calls her name softly, speaks in barely more than a whisper, but Percy starts awake. She has been dreaming that she is dancing with Mrs. Miller, who wore no blouse, only a lacy camisole through which Percy could clearly see the dark outline of her nipples.

Mrs. Miller touches Percy's shoulder. Honey, we're home. I didn't know we'd be so late.

Percy sits up. She feels fuzzy-headed and sheepish, as if Mrs. Miller might somehow know what she has been dreaming. She has often imagined herself in Mr. Miller's arms, and although she is a little frightened about what might happen next, she senses it would be easy enough to make the fantasy real. But this is different.

She stares openly as Mrs. Miller slides her jacket off her shoulders, notices the lithe arch of Mrs. Miller's torso as she shakes free of her coat sleeves and the way her neck stretches in an elegant curve. Percy lowers her eyes. Suppose Mrs. Miller *is* a lesbian? Does that give Percy any right to stare at her breasts and imagine them soft and naked?

When Percy dares to look again, she forces her eyes to remain on Mrs. Miller's face, an act she hopes will appear more natural than it feels.

Even by Percy's standards, Pamela Miller is still young, much younger than Percy's mother, and she has an average build, nothing particularly big or small. She wears black slacks with a simple red sweater, and her face is kind as she smiles at Percy.

Did everything go okay? Did Derek go to sleep all right?

I gave him some milk, and rocked him, then he slept the whole time.

Mrs. Miller smooths Percy's hair. Sadly, her touch feels no different than it ever has.

That's good, honey. I'll go look in on him, but you see
Dan. He'll pay you.

Percy nods and rises. Her body aches, and all she wants is
her bed and more sleep. Feeling a bit grumpy, she looks at
Mrs. Miller again. She appears no different than she ever
has. So far as Percy can see, there is nothing weird about her
at all.

DURING the summer, Percy and Marlea are in the bus as much as they are out of it, and until this year, Percy's older brother Bobby has never bothered them. But now that they are going into high school, he has begun to hover around, usually with two or three friends in tow. Percy, however, is adamant that neither Bobby nor his friends will intrude on the time she spends with Marlea. She pushes the sturdy metal lever to lock the boys out of the bus, then double-checks the wide rubber seal to make certain there is no way Bobby can slip his arm in and pry the door open.

Even so, the boys bang on the outside of the bus and flatten their faces against any window left uncovered.

Priscilla, Bobby says, let us in and we'll share our cigarettes.

Never! And as you know, my name is Percy.

Prissy, let us in. Come on.

Percy slides the window down and open. Give me a cigarette anyway, or I'll tell.

He throws her a scornful look. As if he cares what she tells. He is nearly seventeen, and his hair is long and shaggy, his dress careless. Their parents know that he smokes cigarettes but not that he prefers pot, when he can get it. C'mon, he says. I'll give you as many as you want when you let us in.

She reaches down and hooks her fingers into Bobby's nostrils, looks around to make sure his friends get the message as well. She stretches his head up until he stands on tiptoes, and she stares him down. Instead of raising her voice, she lowers it, for effect. If you can't call me by my name, she says, you'll never get inside.

Before he can retaliate, she unhooks her fingers and snaps the window closed. His friends fall over themselves laughing. They pull their nostrils up and stare at the sky, imitating Bobby, but he only shakes his head, rubs his nose a bit, and laughs along with them.

Bobby likes to laugh, and he often reads parts of the newspaper for the amusement of his friends. *Fire resistant gun for sale,* he says, miming a hunter who can't get his gun to fire. Won't shoot worth a damn, but it's a great poker for the campfire. He grins at them. How long do you think it'll take the guy to sell that one?

Or listen to this, he says. *Buick LeSabre, $3,500. Ford pickup, $2,000.* He runs down the list of ads. Here's the good one: *Oldsmobile Cutlass: Stolen. Please return ASAP.* Nothing down, he says. No interest. Don't pay until you get caught.

Marlea laughs hardest of all. I wish I had a brother, she says.

Percy feels a paring knife scrape at the lining of her stomach. You can have him, she says, her tone petulant. Nothing down. Don't pay until you get caught.

She notices that whenever Bobby makes a joke, he always looks in Marlea's direction to see if she is laughing, and that when Marlea comes to their trailer, Bobby disappears into the washroom and makes an entrance a few minutes later with his shaggy hair brushed back. If Marlea wears makeup, if she wears a new shirt or even washes her hair, Bobby comments on her appearance or on the way she smells. But Percy is also aware that Marlea seems oblivious to these clues.

Marlea is an only child, and Percy can see that her parents adore her. Her mother supports her opinions no matter what, her father praises her for having them, and they both hug and cuddle her every chance they get. If someone compliments Percy, she thinks about the compliment, and what it might mean, for days, but when Bobby compliments Marlea, she accepts the praise as nonchalantly as she accepts it from anyone else. Percy wants to see that that never changes.

When she sees Bobby admiring Marlea's heavy new pendant, nothing between his sweaty hand and her breasts but a thin T-shirt and a few lacy strips of bra, Percy decides she has heard enough. She waits until she and Bobby are kneeling on the ground collecting worms from the flower bed. They have put their catch in paper cups—ten or twelve pinkish wrigglers in each cup, ready to sell to the grocery store for bait. They get twenty-five cents a cup, and they can usually make three or four dollars. But just as Percy is about to question Bobby, Mr. Turner pads outside in his slippers. He walks to the gate where the sidewalk blocks end and directs a malevolent stare at the Dunns' trailer, so similar to his own. When he turns back, he acknowledges his children.

One of the reasons why I would never own a welding truck, he says, just as if they have asked, is that damn Dunn. He's out of town more often than he's home. He lays a hand on each of their heads. It's easy to be a hero when you've got a fat wallet. Specially when you can up and run off whenever you like.

To punctuate his remark, he horks a wad from his throat and spits forcefully off to the side. You remember that when you're feeling hard done by.

He looks as if he might have more to say, but in the end he merely nods his head a few times and shuffles up the steps into the porch, leaving his children staring after him.

Percy sees her opportunity. She turns to Bobby and rests her hand on his head. She makes her voice stern like her

father's. One of the reasons why I still like you, she says, is
that you haven't tried to steal my best friend.

She plans to say more, but Bobby stops her by copying
her movement and placing his own hand on her head.

He waits until she looks directly at him. What makes you
think she's yours to steal?

Percy glares at him. We've always been friends.

So?

She shoves him. Don't think I don't see you prissing
yourself up—

Don't push me.

She pushes him again. I'll do more than push you—

Wait a minute, Bobby says. He holds his hands up and
grins. I'm just saying that you don't own her.

Percy scoops a handful of dirt from the flower bed and
throws it at him. Maybe not, but if you even think of kissing
her, I'll cut your lips off.

WHEN she is fifteen, Percy grows tired of protecting her virginity like some mark of distinction that is supposed to, but doesn't, give her status. In health class, while most of her friends giggle and try to feel each other up in the dark, she listens to what the scratchy film voice says about ovaries, about testicles. The drawings are pink, like the one pinned to the wall in the doctor's office, and seem entirely unrelated to her body. She sneaks free pamphlets from the drugstore into her school textbooks, reads every word about diaphragms, condoms made from latex and sheep gut, about jellies and pills. When she decides, she calls to set up an appointment with Dr. Hill.

And what do you want to see Dr. Hill about? the receptionist asks.

Percy's throat clenches shut and she can't answer, doesn't want to. What if she hadn't telephoned, but had walked into the clinic and approached the receptionist in person?

Miss? Are you there? Do you wish to make an appointment?

I want to talk about the pill.

Are you using contraceptives now?

Yes, she lies.

The internal examination is Percy's first.

Slide your bottom down a bit more, Dr. Hill says. No, more than that. Come on, right down to the end. Thatagirl, don't be shy.

Percy's buttocks are even with the edge of the examining table, practically even with the stirrups holding her feet steady on both sides of the table. Her legs, folded like wings, flop easily when Dr. Hill pushes them open wider. He rolls forward on a low stool.

The last time Percy readied the inside of the Christmas turkey for dressing, she rinsed the cavity under the tap according to her mother's direction, rubbed salt against the ribs, and then peered inside. Any minute now, she expects the doctor to produce a salt shaker and start rubbing.

If she opens her mouth, she's certain she'll find a white paper bag filled with bloody turkey gizzard, liver, and a heart. She feels herself gag and makes a slight choking sound just as the speculum slides in.

Relax, says Dr. Hill. This might be a bit chilly, but it won't hurt.

The metal speculum does hurt as it pushes on the walls of her vagina, and she endures the bite of the swab with a sharp intake of breath.

She wants to flap her wings and catch the doctor's head between her thighs—his head that is down there some- where, if only she could see through the sheet that separates her from the bottom half of her body and causes her to feel like a private peep-theatre for the doctor. He sounds perky enough. *Thatagirl. Don't be shy.*

Percy's legs react quickly. Like springs pushed too far back, they release all at once and snap shut, clamp Dr. Hill's head between her thighs. She feels, rather than hears, the vibration of his screams on her vulva as she reaches down and stretches her labia over his ears. His voice, muffled by her flesh, is no longer authoritative and unconcerned. With his nose pressed against her clitoris, he speaks into her vagina like a megaphone, the sounds amplified into her chest: *Let me out of here. Next time I'll warm the specu-lum. I'll drop the sheet and keep your legs closer together. I promise.* And then the echo: *I promise. I promise.*

How're you doing, Priscilla?

Percy waits until Dr. Hill pulls the instrument out. Her vagina closes with a slippery pop. Her hands are icy wet, her face red. I'm okay, but it's Percy. My name is Percy.

BRADLEY writes poems to Percy during class and copies her homework in his notebook after school. *The earth is full of secrets*, he writes, *kept until we can hear them together.* He is short and soft, like a comfortable pillow, and whenever he props himself in the corner of the old davenport in his parents' basement, Percy cuddles into him, partly because she likes the feel of him, and partly to keep warm. The basement is unfinished and damp, and it is here that he first touches her developing breasts, sucks on them gently, and tries to convince Percy to go all the way. Six weeks after her visit to the doctor, when Bradley slides his fingers inside her panties, she is ready.

I want to do it, she says. Inside her socks, her toes feel clammy and cold. Her days of virginity are over, and Bradley will be the first. His father has an out-of-town sales route, and his mother bowls in a league every Wednesday. Percy saw the note pinned to the refrigerator when they came in—Cold cuts and salad in the fridge. See you at eight.

This morning Percy planned ahead, took her new panties—bought secretly and especially for this occasion—to school and wore her best bra. Her mother thinks she has a music practice, and Marlea will vouch that it is true. All week she has been thinking about how she will tell Bradley, watching him, deciding whether she *will* tell him, reserving the right to change her mind. At school today, he slacked off in gym class and had to run circles while the rest of the class watched. When she witnessed his puffy, red-faced humiliation, she felt sorry for him and decided right then. She wouldn't change her mind.

The way Brad's eyes widen, she might have handed him a hundred-dollar bill. For a moment he looks unsure, then he pulls himself together and releases the latch on the davenport so that it flops open into a bed. He struggles out of his jeans, and stands before Percy clad only in bright white undershorts.

His legs look soft and freckled, and this, along with the newness of his underwear, heightens her interest. She has only seen his legs in long gym shorts, and she has imagined him in underwear similar to her brother's—dull, faded Stanfields strung from his hips with stretched elastic—but Brad's underwear fits snugly, is pouchy in front and looks full of promise. His eyes don't know where to look.

Are you sure? he asks.

Percy lifts her hips, and he tugs on the legs of her jeans. Together they dispense with both her jeans and the expensive new panties. Red. With lace, to signify love. They have talked about this moment, have agreed to go slow, to make the first time as easy as possible.

Now, perhaps because he is confronted with so much flesh all at once, Brad's hands hover over her, graze her shoulders and breasts. You're so smooth, he says. He kicks the knob on the TV with his foot, and the sound of World Wrestling is replaced with an even more unsettling silence.

Take off your shorts, Percy says, and Bradley does.

Then, as if to cover himself, or because he is afraid she might change her mind, he gently spreads her legs and prods until he finds his way inside.

Are you okay? he asks. He glances at her face, then back down at his penis, visible, then not.

Percy nods, bright-eyed, eager for intercourse. Except with Marlea, she doesn't like to show her body, but she lifts her hips for Bradley with only the slightest hesitation. She doesn't expect the entry to be so easy, so painless, and except for when he pulls a few pubic hairs, she experiences no discomfort, only a warm, urgent feeling as she rocks against him. She watches, interested, as his face contorts.

Close your eyes, he says.

When he finishes, Percy pushes him aside and uses his shirt to wipe herself.

You can't look, he says. You're not supposed to look.

I don't see why not. And then, touching herself the way she has learned to, she adds, you can look at me if you want.

For a minute he does, then he rolls to face the basement wall. I don't want to, he says. It's not right.

It's okay, I still love you, he says later.

It doesn't occur to Percy to question his forgiveness. Instead, she imagines herself making him happy, cooking his dinner and ironing his clothes. She isn't certain she will be satisfied doing all those things she normally hates, but she thinks being a wife is probably something she'll adapt to, once it is expected of her, the way she once liked memorizing Bible verses to please her Sunday School teacher.

They will wait two and a half more years until graduation and then marry right away, she tells Marlea, and although she secretly wonders if there is something more to sex, or why everyone makes such a big deal of it if there isn't, she doesn't mind that the only orgasms she has are those she gives herself. She is content to curl against Brad's soft stomach, and when she tenderly wipes sweat from his forehead, she honestly believes they will be together forever.

When he tells her that she shouldn't touch herself so much, she voices no objections.

It's not right, he says, after the second time. Not if you're decent. So she waits until he goes to the bathroom for a towel, and she touches herself then.

When she was babysitting for Mr. and Mrs. Miller, she found *The Happy Hooker* on a shelf behind some other books, and she read the entire book in two sittings. But when she places her finger on Brad's anus and runs her teeth along his penis, he leaps up.

What the hell are you doing? He points to his shrivelled penis. Why can't you be normal and stop acting like a whore?

She isn't sure he knows anything about whores, but his reproaches take a toll anyway, pricking like little cactus stabs of guilt because she is learning from the kind of book that needs to be hidden behind all the others.

When she tries to curl into his back, he pushes her away. Why don't you go home and think about the kind of person you want to be? I don't want to be saddled with a damn whore.

The next day, she knows from his pale, closed face that their time is over. I love you, she writes in a note. She drops it on his desk, but he only balls the message up without reading it and throws it in the garbage from where he sits.

Good shot, someone says, and Percy turns her face to the wall to hide her tears. Then she folds the rest of her thoughts inside herself, where they can't get tossed out. Until now, Marlea has heard almost every detail, but never have the details made Percy look this bad.

When Marlea asks, Percy just shakes her head. I'll tell you later, she says, and after a while, the thought of telling Marlea everything, even that she has acted like a whore, comforts her.

A FEW weeks before Christmas, Percy declines a babysitting job with the Millers. For a while, last summer, she convinced herself that she had only imagined Mr. Miller's interest in her. She had made something out of nothing, her mother would say, had imagined his attention because she had wanted it so badly. But lately the advances have been undeniably overt. The last time she babysat, he stroked her cheek when he said goodbye. The time before that, he lifted her hair when she put on her coat and then kissed her neck.

Don't, Percy said. Although her stomach felt hot and stringy with guilty desire, she wanted to resist.

If you don't like it, I won't, he said. Then he winked and ushered Percy out the door as if he had done nothing at all.

All week Percy has been thinking about Mr. Miller, and she has decided that Uncle George was right. Once trouble finds you, you're sunk.

I'm sorry, she says into the phone, but I'm already booked for New Year's Eve. She keeps her voice low and angles her body into the wall as she speaks, but it is no use. Her mother hears.

What do you mean you're already babysitting? I don't know about any babysitting. Who was that?

Pamela Miller, Percy says. I told her I can't babysit.

You lied?

Mom. I told you. I don't like them. I feel uncomfortable there.

And I told *you,* Mrs. Turner says, extending the telephone to Percy. You don't have to like them to take their money when they offer it. We're not rolling in dough here, Percy.

Except for this interference by her mother, Percy might have been successful in her plan to avoid Mr. Miller. Instead, she is sprawled, half-asleep, on the Millers' couch when they return at two in the morning.

Happy New Year, Percy! Mrs. Miller looks red around the eyes, and tired, but she smiles brightly. I saved this for you.

She holds a small cardboard box, a silver rectangle, simply decorated. Here, she says. Truffles. They came with champagne at midnight—

Truffles? Percy says. Thank you.

When Mrs. Miller leaves to check on Derek, Percy opens the box and looks inside. Apparently a truffle is something to be happy about. There are four, iced and separated by layers of silver and gold foil. She pokes her nose forward and catches the aroma of rich chocolate. With deliberate care, she places the box inside her purse, then bends to look at a photograph of Derek sitting under the Christmas tree.

Through the soles of her stocking feet, she feels the floor shiver with the approach of Mr. Miller. His step is quiet and he places a finger to his lips. He wears dress slacks and a deep green sweater over a shirt and tie. Percy has never seen anyone more handsome.

Hey, he whispers. Everybody got a New Year's hug except you. He opens his arms and she doesn't hesitate. She walks right in.

He kisses her then. Not a friendly, perfunctory greeting, but an intense adult kiss, his insistent tongue separating her lips in a way she has never imagined. She immediately feels more desire than she ever experienced with Brad. This time, she is kissing a *man*, and her whole body answers. She feels neither guilt nor fear, only a desire to continue this heated kissing for a very long time.

Mr. Miller breaks away first. Wow, he says, keeping his arms around her. Happy New Year.

Percy is unsure how to act now that they are no longer clamped together. Suddenly he is Mr. Miller, father and husband once again, and she wishes he had never broken away. Happy New Year, she says. She is anything but happy. As much as she has fantasized about this moment, she can't enjoy it. He is drunk. He has to be. And anyway, she is betraying Mrs. Miller's trust just as Mrs. Miller has begun to treat her as a friend.

But what if Mrs. Miller *is* a lesbian? That would make everything okay, wouldn't it? If Marlea is right, and Mrs. Miller wants other women, then it would only be normal for Mr. Miller to want someone too.

His arm still supports Percy in a loose hug. You have such beautiful hair, he says. Such colour.

Percy can't discern whether he is sincere or not. No one has ever suggested that her hair is anything but an unruly mess. No, that isn't entirely true. Once, after sex on his parents' couch, Brad said that he liked the way her hair curled in every direction. But he didn't express himself the way Mr. Miller just did, low and sexy. Growly, and grown-up.

There's a twenty in my pocket for you, by the way. He points at his front pants pocket. This one.

A twenty! You only owe me ten. From seven until midnight, then double pay until now.

He places his finger to his lips again. Sshh. Just take it.

She hears his breathing nearly stop as she digs in his pocket. Her fingers close around a folded bill, and then they brush against the hard shape of his erection. She feels, as well as hears, his intake of breath.

He pulls her into the front entry and kisses her again.

Where's Pamela? Percy asks.

Bed, he says, silencing her with his mouth. This time, with her back pressed to the wall, she feels the whole length of him against her. He pulls back for a second and unzips his fly, exposing himself.

There's another twenty in my other pocket if you'll touch me, he says. He places her hand where he wants it and looks down. She looks too. She has no qualms about touching him. She'd get naked and lie with him, right here on the floor, if Mrs. Miller wasn't just down the hall.

Pinch me, he says.

What? Percy asks, startled. She has heard him clearly enough, but she is unsure what he means.

Pinch me, he repeats. He takes her fingers and squeezes them on his testicles. Pinch me hard. Hurt me, he says. His eyes plead with her as he offers her a second twenty dollar bill.

Percy doesn't have sex with Dan Miller, not in the ordinary sense. He takes her to a holiday trailer parked on a site off in the woods, a small damp affair with walls buckling and water stains around both ceiling vents.

The land is mine, Dan says. Ten acres, and I cleared this patch myself last year. Someday I'll build on it, or maybe just move the double-wide here.

Percy nods. That'd be nice for Derek.

Dan shakes his head and holds his finger to her lips. It's nice because there's nobody here but us. We don't even need to mention them. He tosses her a bag. For you.

He brings her inexpensive but beautiful gifts. Today it is a chocolate heart. Over the past few weeks he has given her others—six thin stalks of lavender wound tightly together with a strip of satin ribbon, a round of amber hanging by a thread, thin slices of orange dried to resemble stained glass. They are thoughtful gifts she can take home with little difficulty. She made them in craft class, she will say if she has to.

He gives her money too, but after the first time he is careful about when and how he gives it to her. You look like you need a new jacket, he says one time. I'll give you extra when you babysit next week.

And he does. A five in her back pocket when she leaves, an extra ten or twenty in her shoe. That way, they can both pretend that his payment has nothing to do with the barrettes she attaches to his nipples, or the cord she tightens around his testicles before binding his ankles with the remaining length. And although she usually strips to her panties, his arousal has nothing to do with her nakedness.

What excites him is the grovelling he is forced to do, the way she denies him pain until he laps water from a basin on the floor or licks the soles of her feet while she reads aloud from a book he has provided.

He likes her to wear white panties, white knee socks, and white cotton blouses, and to stand perfectly still while he pushes each button through its hole. The first time, he ejaculates before the blouse slides past her shoulders.

Goddammit, he says. Bite me. Bite me hard. He points to his chest, his thighs, his softening penis. Pull my hair too. That's the way. I'm sorry, I'm sorry.

When he first says he's sorry like that, Percy stops pulling his hair, stops biting, and tries to kiss him.

What the fuck are you doing? Hurt me, girl. Don't stop, just hurt me.

Does Pam know about all of this? Percy asks one day. She has skipped classes to spend the afternoon with him, and she doesn't know how she will explain her absence to Marlea. Now she wonders how Dan must feel, lying to Mrs. Miller on a regular basis.

Do you think we'd be here if she did?

Well. She could know.

She doesn't.

Why me, then?

He considers her question for some time before answering. You have a look. The face of an angel and the eyes of a wanton woman.

Percy accepts this, but it startles her because he has chosen to describe her in terms not so different from Brad's complaint that she acts like a whore.

She finds herself looking in the mirror more, trying in vain to discover those details that allow men to be simultaneously attracted and repelled. For she senses that it is the core repulsion that both attracts Dan and allows him to trust her with his guilty needs. Yet beyond her wild hair and amber eyes, she can see nothing that sets her apart.

It is her curiosity, she decides, that has made her suitable. Curiosity and a lack of inhibition are the traits that lead men to suspect a woman of being wanton.

She wishes she could discuss these afternoons with Marlea, but she is afraid that her theory of inhibition will fall apart in Marlea's hands. For the first time she keeps silent, worried that Marlea will see exactly what remains invisible to Percy, but is clearly evident to Brad and Dan. In the end, it is her fear of Marlea's discovery, and Marlea's subsequent repulsion, that causes Percy to say no to more afternoons in the holiday trailer. She cannot keep lying, and she would rather grow horns and a tail than see Marlea turn from her.

THE morning is hot, and Percy wears cut-off blue jeans and a faded cotton blouse. A strip of denim holds her hair off her neck, but stray strands escape the ponytail and fall forward into her face. She knows enough to push these strands back as she goes looking for her mother.

Mom, Percy asks, do you have my birth certificate?

She finds her mother in the bedroom, hot iron in one hand, spray bottle in the other. The windows are open but there is no breeze. A large stack of wrinkled clothes lies heaped on a chair.

Mrs. Turner's face is flushed across the cheeks, and damp. Do I have what?

My birth certificate. The Burger Baron needs someone, so I applied, but I need a social insurance card. For that, I need my birth certificate. Percy holds out the application form.

Mrs. Turner sets the spray bottle on the ironing board and wipes the back of her wrist across her forehead and down one side of her face. She takes the paper, glances at the tiny print, and gives the sheet back to Percy. She looks at her daughter as if she is just seeing her after a very long time. So you want a job, do you?

Percy glances at the pile of ironing. Uh-huh. For pay. Instead of babysitting, I mean. I'm sixteen, Mom. I want a real job.

What you'll get is real *work*. I hope you're prepared for that.

At least I won't be ironing every day of my life, Percy thinks a few minutes later, as she kneels down in the porch.

Somewhere in the trunk, her mother said. That's where she'll find the birth certificate.

The windows here are designed for light, not fresh air, and the heat is oppressive. The trunk itself is too heavy to move, but beautiful, the unpainted metal so long rusted that its surface has taken on an attractive brown patina.

This is the first time she has been allowed to look in the trunk alone, and Percy lifts the bowed lid with care. Inside is a hodgepodge of boxes, fabric, papers, and envelopes. Her mother didn't say where exactly she'd find the birth certificate, so she investigates each item before setting it aside. When she comes across baby books, first Bobby's, then hers, she stops and smiles involuntarily when the pages fall open to a footprint and a curl of red hair.

She strokes the hair tentatively. It is coarse and springy. Even as a baby. The entries taper off after only a few pages. Some weights and measurements, one photo where she looks like an alien in grey tones, long skinny neck, prominent ears, then nothing. Disgruntled to find so little of herself documented, she slaps the covers closed.

Maybe in here, she thinks, and opens a large, unmarked manila envelope. Inside are a number of papers and documents, so she tilts the envelope until the papers slide out.

Right away, a bold headline stands out from the smaller print. MONSTER CHILD BORN TO OLDROCK COUPLE. She lifts the corner of the first page. BABY PRISCILLA DEVIL'S CHILD SAYS MOM.

This has to be something her mother saved because of the name: Priscilla. Or perhaps it is one of those papers Percy has seen advertised in the back of certain magazines—*Make the Headlines on Your Birthday. Any Name Inserted ...* Yet she knows; she can already see a photo of herself. Monster. Devil's child. It says so right here, in the caption under her photo. Her heart pounds in her ears. These stories are about her.

One clipping is longer than the others and printed on glossy paper rather than newsprint. It is the only sheet not noticeably discoloured, and there is a date in the corner. August 1979. Only three years ago. Percy reads this paper first.

Priscilla Turner was an unwanted child. That is, she was longed for until she arrived. Only two weeks after her birth, she and her mother were pictured on the front page of *The Central Star*—an Oldrock weekly. Within days, they were featured in most major newspapers across the country.

The dictates of normal, acceptable behaviour in 1966 reserved no place for mothers to stand by the side of the only highway into town with a placard reading: TAKE THIS CHILD OF THE DEVIL. Had the story happened now, mother and daughter might have appeared on every news program in the nation and probably several talk shows as well. As it was, thankfully, they only made the papers.

Priscilla's mother, Margaret Murphy Turner, believed that her newborn had evil and telepathic powers. *Priscilla was only born*, she was quoted as saying, *to do the work of Satan—to destroy her mother, a devout Christian no longer within Satan's reach.*

Margaret maintained that her hands had been scorched when she lifted her daughter from her makeshift crib— *I've got the blisters to prove it*, she said—and that she had nearly choked on a mouthful of baby talk when, like any normal mother, she cooed words of comfort into her baby's upturned face.

Priscilla's father, Walter Turner, was heard to have

said, *This is all just too much*, but he stood by his wife and family.

Maybe, as some of the more lurid newspapers suggested, this baby was not the most adorable creature ever born, but those three numbers on her little butt—marks Walter said he wouldn't have allowed anyone to photograph—looked more like a blur of musical notes to him, and anyway, *birthmarks aren't unusual*, he said. *My Aunt Martha had a raised patch of purple on her back that you'd swear was nothing other than a giant slug, and people weren't photographing that.* He knew that the abundance of wrinkles on Priscilla's face, along with the stuck-out ears, combined to make her look as if she'd been set in the sun to dry, *but give her a few bottles of milk and she'll plump out soon enough.*

Having children, he said, *is supposed to be one of the happier experiences in a man's life, not a freak show. So I didn't make no calendar baby. That's the least of my worries.*

Clearly, Walter was right about that. In his own words, *How'd you like to have a wife gone crazy and a million loony-tunes popping outta nowhere? How'm I supposed to deal with that and still make a living? You tell me. And all the questions from child welfare workers to boot?*

As far as this reporter can see, Priscilla was no more odd-looking than the average baby. But the papers wanted a story, and this was one they could exploit. According to one article, *those yellow eyes were not inherited from anyone in the family, however far back one checked.* The abundant head of wiry red hair was also uncharacteristic, and apparently did little, when anyone dared to smooth it, to make the infant more sympathetic. Nor did her immediate strength, the way she allegedly flattened her hands against the sides of a glass baby bottle until the fill marks were imprinted on her palms, or the way she was said to gum the rubber nipple right off the end.

This feat in particular was said to frighten her mother. Margaret was frail and thin and had nursed her baby for only three days before she allegedly screamed out in terror. When a nurse came running, she found Margaret struggling to pry Priscilla's jaws apart. With her fingers jammed into Priscilla's mouth, Margaret is said to have *pulled up with her right arm and down with her left. When finally her nipple slid free, Margaret dumped Priscilla aside and tended to her wounded breast.* Either she never noticed or didn't care, the papers reported, that the nurse had to catch Priscilla in mid-air when she rolled past the edge of the hospital bed. *Get her away from me,* Margaret allegedly screamed, *and don't bring her back.*

Percy cannot immediately digest all that she has just read, but she knows intuitively that she must hide these papers if she ever hopes to see them again. Quickly, she folds the one she has just read and slips it down the seat of her jeans. She hears her mother's footsteps hurrying down the hall, and she must make a decision: hide the rest of the papers or put them back. She has no time to think, and fear wins. She slides the envelope under some others in the trunk and lifts her baby book just as her mother opens the porch door.

Wait, her mother says. Don't be looking through those things. Get away from there.

Percy notices that she is holding the baby book upside down. Before her mother can notice, she sets it back in the trunk and looks up innocently. I thought you said my birth certificate was here.

I know what I said, but I'm not sure. She holds her hand

to her chest and takes a deep breath. It's okay, I'm not mad at you. I just don't want you mucking around in my stuff. I'll get your certificate later, when I'm finished. It'd take you all day to find anything in there.

I don't mind. I'll just look, and then if I don't find it—

I said no! Percy's mother slaps her hand against the wall. Just leave everything the way it is, and I'll put it all back where it belongs later.

Percy can see that there is no point in arguing, and her own insides feel slippery and cold. All *right*, she says as she flounces past, I'll stay away from your precious things.

FOR the rest of the morning and into the afternoon, even when she hears Marlea knock on her door, Percy hides, making a nest for herself in cool, uncut grass growing waist high in the three-foot space between the back fence and the painted chipboard that skirts her parents' trailer. She tramples the grass to make a hideaway and then pulls the article out and reads it over and over. *Devil child. Monster.*

The story makes no sense. She understands the words, the sentences, but strung together the way they are, she thinks there has to be a mistake. Why her? What was so awful and horrible about her that her mother tried to give her away? And why has no one said anything?

At first she cries, but soon the tears dry up, and instead she rips grass from the ground, staining her fingers green. How dare they talk about her behind her back? Or was it *this* guy who made them all remember? She shakes the paper as if she were shaking the reporter by his collar. Is this why people think her mother is a religious nutcake? Do the kids at school know? Does Marlea know?

Percy separates blade after blade from its root, chomping tender, pale stalks down to where the grass leafs out and turns green and sharp like a razorblade. Already she has cut her lip and her fingers accidentally.

Now deliberately, she draws an eight-inch blade of tough green grass across the inside of her arm. Once, twice. She is rewarded by thin red lines of blood that ease out, perfectly straight, as if she has drawn them with a ruler. Over these lines she criss-crosses others until her arm stings painfully. A dull ache in her throat only makes her angrier, and her eyelids feel dry and gritty from staring hard at the paper.

She hears her mother's call and ignores her, wishes her dead, wishes her in hell because she thinks hell is the place her mother fears most. She considers making this nest her home, staying here until everyone is out of the trailer and only then sneaking inside for food and water. If she pries a board away, she can hide under the trailer indefinitely and will never have to face anyone again. Except Marlea will worry, and maybe Mrs. Miller too, when she realizes that Percy's visits have stopped.

At first, Percy felt uncomfortable visiting Pamela Miller, was afraid that Mrs. Miller knew about her trysts with Dan and was only leading up to a confrontation, but this never happened, and Percy's conscience went unrelieved. Humiliating Dan had caused her more bad feelings than good, and when she recalls the time they spent together, she feels loathsome and ugly inside, not only because she regrets betraying Mrs. Miller, but because she wonders what sort of person she is to have found satisfaction in hurting and demeaning him.

It doesn't matter that her own pleasure was fleeting, or that Dan's gratification was genuine. When she degraded him, she felt degraded too. At first her stomach merely tightened and knotted, but later, as she became more creative in the ways she dominated, she felt all choked up in her head. Her thoughts stuck there, aching while she bullied him, but especially afterward, as if all the nasty things she said and did had somehow been redirected inward.

Dan, on the other hand, seemed entirely unaffected. A couple of times he came home to find Percy with Pam, but he acted as if nothing had ever happened between them, so Percy took her cue from him. She pushed the burden of responsibility to the back of her mind and locked it there

while she confided in Mrs. Miller about problems at school
or difficulties with her parents. Sometimes, if Marlea
wasn't with her, she even talked about some of the things
Marlea had told her, trying to confirm the accuracy of facts
that seemed too strange to be true. Did women in some
countries really have to cover their faces when they went
outside? Did most lipstick really contain fish scales?

Now it occurs to Percy that Mrs. Miller may know something more about the article she has found. If Percy is
honest with herself, she would prefer to talk to Marlea, but
Marlea must have known about her mother all along. And
has said nothing! Somehow that seems like the biggest
betrayal of all, and she isn't ready to talk to Marlea just
yet. The way she feels now, she may never speak to her
again.

Instead, she climbs over the back fence and walks straight
to the Millers' trailer, where she tells Mrs. Miller everything. When Mrs. Miller hears the story and reads the article, she sits at the kitchen table and gently strokes Percy's
hair, which hangs in loose, oily curls. She rubs her hand up
and down Percy's back in an attempt to comfort her.

Marlea is your best friend, she says. Even supposing she
heard some version of this story, which she might have,
how could she ask you about it? You may not have believed
her, for starters, and whether you did or not, the story
would have hurt you. The last thing Marlea would want is
to hurt you. She cares about you.

But why would my mom think those things? I still don't
understand.

Mrs. Miller pushes a bowl of caramels across the table
and shakes her head. The article you have is about postpartum depression. I remember the reporter who did it. George
got so mad at him, he punched the guy in the head and

spent a night in jail for it. Some people say that's why George disappeared the way he did. Your dad even called the police and told them to take him away—

Who? The writer, or Uncle George?

The writer. But some of the neighbours talked to him anyway and of course he dug up all the old stories. I would have talked to him myself, but he didn't ask me. He wanted to write a story that would get people to wake up and take notice. No one should have to go through what your mom went through.

But she threw me off the bed! And people tell their kids to stay away from me because of her. They say she's a nutcake.

Look, Percy. I don't know much about the gossip, but I know this. Your mom loves you just as much as I love Derek, and no matter what she said, or how weird it all seems today, she kept you, and she wouldn't *let* anyone take you. That's why you're here now and not in some foster home somewhere. You're old enough to see that.

I haven't told anyone this, but I once suggested to Dan that we give Derek up for adoption. She holds her hand up when Percy tries to object. It didn't seem like a good idea for long, but I was exhausted, and I made the suggestion. Derek was only about three months old, and of course Dan thought I was insane.

Maybe for a few days I was, but everything had changed. I couldn't sleep for more than a few hours at a time, my breasts leaked and hurt, going anywhere was a major event, and suddenly Dan was finding a million reasons to stay out even later than usual. I hated how I looked. I hated my life. I just wanted everything to be as it had been. Do you understand?

Percy nods. I think so.

That was postpartum depression too, and it's not uncommon. It's the same for your mom. She probably didn't even know what she was saying.

Percy nods again. She has only now noticed that Mrs. Miller is still rubbing her back. I guess, she says.

Mrs. Miller's hand feels warm and strong through Percy's thin blouse, and this time her touch makes Percy's skin all quivery everywhere. She also notices Mrs. Miller's smooth brown leg pressing against her own bare one, and she doesn't know whether this is intentional or just the natural result of sitting so close. She wants to reach out and touch that tanned skin, but she is afraid that doing so will make Mrs. Miller send her home. She puts her head on her arms and hopes that Mrs. Miller will not stop, but will continue to caress her for a long, long time. She doesn't.

Mrs. Miller reaches for a cigarette, opens the pack, and pulls one out. She wears rings on most of her fingers, so when she lights up, Percy sees an opportunity to reach for her hand.

I love your rings.

Mrs. Miller looks hard at Percy. I like rings, she says.

I like this one the best. Percy traces the outline of a gold squiggle on a wide band worn on Mrs. Miller's right hand. Her face burns. She is sure she is acting like an idiot, but she doesn't know how to stop now that she has begun. For all of her experimentation with sex, she has given little thought to the subtleties of seduction.

On the other hand, she does know one way to get attention. Percy drops Mrs. Miller's hand and stands. In one quick motion, she raises her blouse over her head and drops it to the floor. The day is sweltering, and she wears no brassiere; her eyes are defiant, and they plead. Resist me now, they say.

Mrs. Miller is about to draw on her cigarette. She stops

with her lips still open and moves to set her cigarette in the ashtray, but she misses the slot and the burning cigarette rolls onto the table. She picks it up and stabs it into the ashtray so that it breaks and tobacco spills out. She stands quickly and steps close to Percy.

My God. Look at you! She grabs Percy's arm and holds it out. What have you been doing to yourself? She gently tugs Percy over to the sink, where she pulls a clean cloth from a drawer, wets it, and wipes the dried blood from Percy's forearm.

She opens her arms and embraces Percy, holds her head against her own shoulder the way she would hold Derek if he were screaming his lungs out, one hand cupping the back of Percy's head, the other stroking her cheek. Even with Percy naked, there is nothing erotic in the gesture. Oh, Percy, she says.

At first Percy tries to pull away. She wants to lash out, to force everything out into the open by saying that Dan is happy enough to see her naked, why isn't she? But Mrs. Miller has never been anything but kind to her. She lets her head fall against Mrs. Miller's shoulder and all the anguish she has been holding in her stomach spills out.

When Percy's sobs stop, Mrs. Miller steps back. Wait here, she says. I'll get you something.

Percy snatches her blouse from the floor and quickly covers herself.

Mrs. Miller returns with an antiseptic cream. This is all I have, she says, but you should get some Mercurochrome or something to fix that up. She pushes Percy's sleeve up and dabs the cream on her arm, spreading it carefully. Then she holds Percy's shoulders and looks into her eyes. Oh honey, are you okay? I'm worried about you. Have you done this before?

Percy shakes her head no, and Mrs. Miller sighs heavily. Well, don't do it again, okay? You had me scared there.

She brings a jug of lemonade to the table and pours each of them a glass. About your blouse—

Percy blushes deep red. I'm sorry. That was stupid. I just thought ... She stops, not quite able to say.

Mrs. Miller waits, then she takes Percy's hand. Have you and Marlea ...? She too allows the question to trail off. She releases Percy's hand in order to open her own, palm upward, in a helpless gesture.

Percy looks stricken. She shakes her head emphatically. I want to touch her all the time, but I've never told her that. She'd hate me if she knew—

No. No, she wouldn't. Mrs. Miller sounds absolutely certain. She'll never hate you, Percy, anyone can see that. And it's possible ... I mean ... have you ever thought that she might feel the same way about you?

I don't think so, says Percy. But how do you *know*? I need to know.

DID you know about this? Percy asks. She and Marlea are safely locked in the bus. She has given Marlea time to read the article, but her time is up. Did you know? She doesn't mean to sound as angry as she does, but her question has a harshness she can't take back.

Marlea shakes her head. No. None of it. She goes pale, then sucks in a breath and turns bright pink. I mean, some of it, but not all this stuff about you. Only that your mom went kind of nuts for a while after she had you. Sometimes people say she's still nuts. Marlea looks frightened then, as if she has said too much.

For a moment, Percy hates her mother. Then she feels an urge to slug Marlea for what she has just said. My mother's not crazy, she says, glaring.

For the first time in a long while, she remembers Susan Martin's voice in the change room—*You don't really like her, do you?*—and Marlea's answer. *Yeah. I don't know.*

Her voice rises. If you're really my friend, you should tell me what you've heard. It's no big secret. Everybody else seems to know all about me. So how come you can't tell me? She leans close to Marlea and yells in her face. Do you think I'm crazy too?

Marlea's composure crumbles under Percy's attack. Don't yell at me, she says. Her shoulders shake and she talks through her tears, her eyes wide and frightened. My mom says that if I talk about it, I'm no better than any other gossip in this town. She says there isn't any of it that won't make you feel bad.

I'm sorry, Percy yells. Goddammit, I'm sorry, okay? She

glares at Marlea, then slumps down beside her on the bunk.
She puts her arm around Marlea and lowers her voice. I'm
sorry. Really. I didn't mean to make you cry. But I can't
stand all these secrets. Just tell me what you've heard.
Please.

Marlea wipes her nose and eyes with her hand. What did
your mom say?

She doesn't know yet. I was going to tell her after I talked
to you.

You haven't told her? She's been outside calling you.
And she came over here. She didn't sound too happy.

We'll see how she sounds when I show her this, Percy
says. She takes the article back from Marlea and returns it
to her pocket. Mrs. Miller says the neighbours talked to this
writer guy. Maybe he talked to your mom too.

Well, I didn't hear that. My mom just said what Mrs.
Miller said. That your mom got sick. And that she was
really poor and thought she could get money from people if
she got enough attention.

Really? This is news to Percy, but her tone is sceptical.
Why would anyone give her money for trying to pass me
off as some evil monster?

I'm not sure. My mom didn't say if she *got* any money,
only that she might have thought she could.

Well. At least that's something I can ask about.

What did Bobby say?

I saw him on my way here, and he was weird. I think he
was stoned. He said she won't talk about it, but it's the
reason why she's always clipping Jesus stories. It's guilt, he
said. She's scared Jesus doesn't want her, so she'll do
anything. That's why people get crazy about Jesus, he said.
They're trying to find a way to get rid of the guilt.

Then he tried to be funny. If it's true, he said, if I really am a devil child, I can show him and all his friends around hell when they get there, and just think—no more cold winters. Stuff like that. He said they're all crazy. Dad's got his head up his ass, and Uncle George is a prick, literally, whatever that means, and Mom's got the whole fucking town talking about us. He told me I should just forget it, that it doesn't matter. And I'm sure it doesn't, to him. He's not the one my mom was trying to get rid of. Percy covers her face with her hands and tries to blink the tears away.

Marlea pulls Percy's hands from her face. Don't hide your face. Why do you always hide your face when you cry?

Because I'm ugly. Percy swallows hard and allows Marlea to look at her. I'm ugly when I cry.

No, you're not. You're never ugly. You're beautiful, and fun, and the best friend anyone could have.

I thought you might like me less now. Because of my mom and everything.

Marlea squeezes Percy around the waist. Are you nuts? She covers her hand with her mouth. Oh God. I'm sorry. I didn't mean—

But Percy bursts out laughing. Somehow it doesn't matter quite so much what her mother did all those years ago if Marlea thinks she is beautiful, and fun, and the best friend anyone could have.

It's okay. You don't have to watch everything you say around me. That was kind of funny.

Then they are both laughing, and Percy feels happier than she has in a very long time.

We're friends forever, Marlea says. D'you hear? She smiles such a loving, sweet smile that all Percy's usual feelings of desire for her are tripled in one instant.

I love you, Percy says fiercely.

I love you too.

They fall back on the bunk and hug each other tightly, like lovers. They kiss like lovers too, naturally, as if it is the way all friends kiss, even using their tongues.

Marlea, Percy thinks, seems just as eager as she is. Still, she doesn't touch Marlea as she wants to but only luxuriates in the feel of Marlea's arms tight around her as they lie there, not saying anything at all about the kiss, just holding each other and grinning as if they have nothing better to do than spend the whole day pressed as close as pages in a book. This is better than anything Percy felt with Brad. Better, by far, than her time with Dan.

Hey, Marlea says suddenly. Maybe the library has copies of the newspapers from when you were born.

Percy sits up, shaking off the dark feelings that have begun to return. Now that's an idea. Will you help me?

Before this, neither of them has researched any topic using more than the encyclopedia, so they tell the librarian that they are interested in headlines from July and August 1966. Before long they are seated at a large wooden table stacked with newspapers from around the country.

The first paper Percy looks through is *The Red Deer Advocate*, dated July 10, 1966. Her birthday. The front page story catches her eye. UNDERGROUND FIRE FRIGHTENS FARMER.

Look at this, she says, reading the story aloud. *Flames lick up out of the earth on Lucifer Black's farm near Delburne.* She grins at Marlea. His name is Lucifer? They've got to be kidding.

Crowds from miles around gather to stare and wonder.

I don't understand it, said Black. There are dry leaves and grass everywhere. Flames jump out the earth six or eight inches high. It looks like the fire is burning from the inside out.

It's hell, Percy says seriously. This must be where I was born. In hell with Lucifer. She laughs too hard, and soon she is covering her face again. I don't know why I'm crying. It's funny. It really is.

She pulls herself together and continues reading. *While dozens have turned up to puzzle, many wonder if they are seeing the beginning of the end.* For a fire is kindled in mine anger, and shall burn unto the lowest hell, and shall consume the earth with her increase, *one old-timer quoted volubly from Deuteronomy. Others believe the fire is caused by spontaneous combustion of underground stores of charcoal.*

According to Black, he is afraid for the safety of his family. The fire is bad enough, says Black, but a few extremists are drawing attention to my name and making connections that frighten me.

This is even more bizarre than my mom, Percy says. I have to keep this.

She takes the paper to the librarian and asks if she can make a duplicate. She returns triumphant. Look, she says, waving a copy of the story. I'm going to start a scrapbook about underground fire. Maybe there really is heaven and hell.

It doesn't take long to find headlines similar to the ones Percy has already seen. BABY PRISCILLA DEVIL'S CHILD SAYS MOM.

Here's one, Percy says. Her face flushes pink, and her eyes blur as she reads. They find several others, but she doesn't learn anything new. The same information has been recycled in a dozen different ways in each of the articles. After about an hour of searching, Marlea finds something else.

She pushes *The Central Star* in front of Percy. This one mentions money.

The story reports that a group of local church women started a fund in support of Percy's parents. At first there were a few donations of second-hand clothing and food, but the story became noteworthy when a local trailer manufacturer offered the Turners a trailer with nothing down and low interest for fifteen years. Then there were offerings from diaper services and cases of baby food and formula. One photo shows a wan but grateful-looking Mrs. Turner smiling into the camera from a hospital bed. Piled around her are toys and baby clothes.

Jesus! Percy says. I'm no devil child. I'm a fairy goddaughter. She can't determine whether the feelings churning inside are happiness for her parents or mortification at their notoriety. As far as Percy can tell, circumstances began looking up for her parents after her birth.

I CAN imagine all sorts of reasons why they might not like to talk about it, says Marlea's mom, but if you're going to keep digging up articles and asking questions, I might as well tell you what I know. We hadn't even moved here when you were born, of course, but it's not like I haven't heard the stories. Your mother's version too, once.

My mom talked to you?

Not exactly. She brought this letter over one day, and left it with me. You can have it if you like. Mrs. Dunn smooths a letter open on the table. She's never been very friendly, Percy, but I don't hold it against her. It's because of all the gossip she's had to put up with.

Percy nods. Maybe, she thinks, but she's not so sure her mother would ever like Marlea's mom. Mrs. Dunn isn't serious enough, for one thing, and besides, her mom doesn't seem to *want* friends. She skims the letter silently, then reads it aloud for Marlea's benefit.

Dear Mrs. Dunn, I see people going in and out of your trailer, and I know that you are hearing all kinds of stories about me. Your daughter and my daughter are friends, and I suppose that's all right, but I don't want your daughter telling mine a pack of lies. That's why I'm writing to you. To set the record straight.

When Percy was born, I had a nervous breakdown. Later, I was in hospital for nearly a month and had drugs and electric shock treatments. That much is true. Also that I did some strange things while I was out of my normal head. Like try to give her away. As a mother yourself, I hope you understand. I am ashamed and I don't want Percy to hear of these things, at least not until she is older and has a better chance of understanding.

I didn't pretend to be sick to get ahead in life, and if any of those big mouth gossips ever had shock treatments they'd be singing a different tune. Do you think I'd get shock treatments in the hope people would be kind? I don't think so. I had no way of knowing anything good would happen. I was sick, but I don't want my kids hurt just because I was.

Please make sure you don't add to the lies.

Percy is the first to break the awkward silence that accompanies the end of her reading. Wow, she says. I had no idea. So what was everyone saying? Were they mad about all the stuff we got? Like the trailer? She is beginning to feel as if she will never understand. Each partial answer only leads to more questions.

Mrs. Dunn shrugs helplessly. You'll have to ask your mom if there's anything else. I told you I'd tell you what I know, and what I know is that your mother gave me this letter. Anything else I've heard is gossip, no one version like any other.

I guess. Percy's voice is sullen. I still don't get it.

Mrs. Dunn rises suddenly. She comes around the table and pulls Percy into her arms where she rocks her in a gentle hug. I'm not sure you'll ever get it, sweetie. Your mother suffered after you were born, and she's probably suffering right this minute, but that doesn't mean she's ever going to give you the answers you want.

But—

And sometimes, Mrs. Dunn says, stopping Percy, that's all for the best. Sometimes answers are more trouble than they're worth.

I T is nearly five o'clock when Percy finally returns home. The instant she walks in the door, her mother is there.

Where on earth have you been? She takes Percy by the arm and hustles her down the hall into the living room. Answer me. Where have you been?

Get your hands off me, Percy says coldly.

Mrs. Turner tightens her grip. I don't know what you think you're up to—

I *said*, get your fucking hands off me.

Mrs. Turner pulls Percy around to face her. Her cheeks have flushed and her eyes are black pinpoints of anger. She has Percy by both shoulders, and she shakes her as she speaks. So long as you're in this house, you're going to show some respect—

Jesus fuck shit goddamn fucking Jesus bitch. Fuck you. Percy glares at her mother, focusing on her tight lips, and deliberately pushes the expletives past her own tongue, dropping each word into the room as a separate act of defiance. With a quick, sharp move that Bobby taught her, she snaps both arms outward and her mother's grip on her shoulders is broken.

Mrs. Turner reacts just as quickly. She raises her arm and slaps Percy so hard that her head turns sideways.

Percy grabs a small three-legged footstool, and holds it between her and her mother.

Fuck Jesus, fuck Jesus, fuck Jesus. Shit fucking cunt Jesus shit fuck.

Mrs. Turner backs away, and a look of offended disbelief replaces her angry expression. In the narrow trailer there is little room to back away far, so when her legs touch the sofa, she reaches out a hand to steady herself and abruptly sits. She glances quickly at the clock on the wall and then folds her arms over her chest.

I don't know what you think you're doing, but you're lucky your father isn't home to see it. You'd be over the bed with the strap by now. She pauses, then she makes her voice rational, almost conciliatory. Do you want to tell me why you're acting like this?

Percy can see in her mother's eyes that she is confused and afraid, and her fear gives Percy a small bite of surprised satisfaction. As if you don't know, she says.

Bobby has come up behind Percy, and when he moves into her range of sight, a supportive gesture, she thinks, she sees that his expression is different from their mother's. He is not afraid. Nor is he pretending smug concern.

Show her, he says. Show her what you showed me.

The trailer is still hot, and the screened windows on both sides of the living room are open. Through them, Percy can hear a dog barking and flies bumping against the screen, their flight obstructed. She can hear music coming from the Dunns' trailer, and she wonders if Marlea is listening, waiting to see what she will do next. Maybe Mrs. Dunn is with her, both of them standing quietly, barely breathing, while Percy crosses a line with her mother that no child should cross.

She pulls the folded article from her back pocket and tosses it at her mother, who bends to pick it off the floor. The paper crackles as Mrs. Turner unfolds it and spreads it on her lap. There is no coffee table upon which to lay the paper because there is no room for one. When a table is needed, for company or for her father's tea, a TV tray is snapped onto unstable legs. Bright flowered top. Silver legs.

Cheery, her mother said when she bought them. God knows, we need something cheery.

Percy watches. As soon as her mother sees the paper, her expression loses its smugness, her cheeks their indignant colour. For Percy, this is an admission of wrong, and she waits, but her mother says nothing.

You never wanted me, she accuses. You said I was evil. She still holds the stool in front of her body, her arms as rigid as the rest of her. The room, if it is possible, seems even more quiet than before, her voice unnaturally loud, even under the circumstances. She shakes the stool at her mother. That's not all I saw. I went to the library, and there's a lot more.

Her mother shakes her head slightly and draws her bottom lip into her mouth. She closes her eyes and covers the bottom half of her face with her cupped hand. A tiny mewling sound escapes her, but she seems intent on holding back any reaction at all, as if covering her mouth and closing her eyes will keep everything in, or out. She sets the paper aside and her hand slides up to cover her forehead. Her head is bent and she still shakes it back and forth.

You got this trailer because of me too.

Bobby looks at his sister. Really? I never knew that. How?

Percy whirls on him. What do you care how? All you can do is make jokes. They didn't *want* me! Her voice catches and tears well up in her eyes, but she swallows hard and turns back to her mother. She pokes her mother's knee with the leg of the stool. Say something.

Percy could bring the stool down on her head. That would make her talk. She looks down on her mother's crown and sees that her hair is thinning, that it is no longer shiny and brown. As a little girl she used to comb her mother's hair when she was allowed, and her mother would lean her head back against the couch and smile while Percy stood beside her and smoothed all the shiny strands away from her face. Now the hair is lank and dusty-looking, and only thin streaks of brown give it any colour at all. It is greasy and repulsive, and if only Percy dared, she could grab a thin handful and yank until her mother's face is turned up the way she wants it, saying that somehow everything she has learned is some terrible, ridiculous mistake that happened to some other family. But her mother's head stays bent and silent, and for this, Percy cannot forgive her. She hates her mother more than she has ever hated her before, and there have been plenty of times to hate her in the past.

Once, after church, when Percy lagged behind to pick her mother wild daisies from the long grass running alongside the dusty gravel road, she had almost caught up again when her mother was there beside her, twisting her ear until she screamed.

Look at your shoes, her mother said, still twisting. Just look at them. They used to be white. D'you think shoes don't cost money? D'you think I can just pull them out of a hat? Do you? Finally she released Percy's ear and pushed her forward. You get on home and get those shoes cleaned before I get there.

Or the time the pipes froze for a whole week, and she made Percy bathe in Bobby's bath water.

I peed in it, Bobby said convincingly when he passed her in the hall, and you're going to wash in it.

I don't want to, Percy said, eyeing the cold grey galvanized tub. He peed in it.

Her mother crossed her arms and frowned. Of course he didn't pee in it. Just get in before I give you something to snivel about.

Percy's chin trembled. But I don't want to wash in Bobby's pee.

You'll be washing in more than that if you don't get in there and stop your blubbering. She put her weight on Percy's shoulders and pressed down until Percy was forced to squat, until she could smell the pee that itched into the backs of her knees and stung her buttocks. She hated her mother then, and oh how she hates her now.

She reaches out and prods her mother again, more firmly this time. If you're sorry, you should tell me you're sorry. She stands back and shouts at her mother's silent head. You *should* be sorry.

She pounds the stool on the floor several times, partly to vent her fury, but mostly to frighten her mother into talking. You tried to give me away! You didn't want me!

C'mon, Bobby says. You can see it's not doing any good. She won't talk about it. Let's just leave her alone.

You leave *me* alone, Percy screams. I'm not going anywhere until she talks to me. She throws the stool down, watches it bounce, and then kicks it aside. She reaches down and attempts to lift her mother's head. She puts her hand on her forehead and pushes. Her mother resists.

Sit up, Percy shouts. Sit up and talk to me. Under her hand, her mother's fingers still cover her forehead. They are cold, even in the heat, and for a moment Percy can't breathe. Her mother is dead. The shock has killed her. But she is resisting. Of course she is not dead.

Percy drops to her knees and pushes up on her mother's head with both hands. Get up, she says. Get up right now.

Bobby steps up to Percy and pulls on her arms. C'mon, Percy. This is no better than anything she's done.

Leave me alone, Percy says. Her voice is dangerous and she is determined. She has her mother's head bent back, and she can see that her mother is crying, the tears streaming out from behind closed eyelids.

Stop, her mother says. It is the first word she has spoken, and she says nothing else. Nor does she sit up, but just opens her lips and lets the one word pop out while Percy forces her head back as far as it will go.

Percy is breathing heavily. As far as she is concerned, her mother will sit up and speak or she will snap her head off at the neck. I'll stop when you stop, she says.

Mom, sit up. Bobby's tone is sharp.

Percy can't tell whether he is angry with her or with their mother.

This is crazy, he says. Just sit up.

And suddenly she does. She sits up and Percy falls forward into her lap until she regains her balance and jumps to her feet. Mrs. Turner opens her eyes and sits upright on the couch, making no attempt to stop the tears that run freely down her face.

There's nothing else to say, she says finally. If you've read the papers, there's nothing left to say. I wanted you more than anything, and then finally I had you. It was a terrible time, and I'm so sorry. I love you. I've always loved you.

It is as if the angry torrent has upended itself in Percy, and her rage is lost to a crush of hope. Her mother's face is anguished, something dreadful and tortured, no longer closed and withholding but wide open behind the years of raw disappointment that taught her how to conceal everything that hurt her most. Percy intuits this without words, and if she could articulate what she now recognizes, she would say that she has not been denied love, but only candour. Even if her mother wanted to, Percy is certain she could hide nothing now. She drops to the floor without a second's thought, and the roar in her head subsides. Her own tears wet her mother's knees as she grips her legs to comfort her. They have brushed the bottom of this day together. Whatever they hide in the future, however seldom they speak of love, they have had at least one moment of truth between them.

THE next week, Percy is at the river with Marlea. When they are not closed up in the bus, Percy and Marlea walk to the river to swim and suntan. That is, Marlea swims. Percy won't go near the water except to look for pebbles.

She is sitting on the bank reading a book and wishing she had another cigarette, but mostly she is thinking about that day with her mother. She promised she wouldn't think about it, but she does. She didn't learn as much about her mother as she wanted to, but what she learned about herself is valuable enough. She had never seen her mother cry before, and the terrible empty look of her when she did was enough to make Percy wish she had never forced her to say anything. Seeing her parents cry is more frightening than hating them, she has discovered, worse than wishing them dead, and far worse than deliberately hurting them, because the pain that makes them cry is outside her, something she can't stop on her own.

She sees Marlea coming out of the water, and she waves. How can you swim in that crap? Percy asks. She sets her book aside and points downstream. That's sewage twenty yards away. It's gross. You're going to get some deadly shit disease all over your skin.

Metres, Marlea says, grinning at Percy. You're supposed to say the sewage is only a few *metres* downstream. And notice that we're *upstream* from there. She wipes water from her face and wades out of the river.

Fuck metric, Percy says. And stay away until you get dry. She shades her eyes to see Marlea better. Holy shitteroo, she says.

Now what? Marlea looks down at her swimsuit, a small

smile parting her lips, as if she thinks Percy is merely commenting on her figure. Then, wet and screaming, she stands over Percy. Help me! Get them off!

I told you—

Just help me!

Percy fumbles in her pockets for matches. Her hands tremble. We can burn them, she says. That's supposed to work.

Marlea stands on the bank with her arms and legs outstretched. Shivering, crying, she waits for Percy to do something. How many are there?

One, two. Percy turns Marlea around to see if she has missed any. Three. Four. She looks up. Four, I think. But I'll get them, don't worry.

She lights a match and blows it out. Her initial sharp, jabbing motion with the hot match head makes no difference to the leech on Marlea's hip. It flinches, but stays put.

Marlea sniffles and wipes her nose with her fingers. Maybe you have to do it slower.

Yeah. Probably. Percy lights another match and tries again. This time she grinds the match head into the middle of the leech, holding the match steady until both pointy ends of the leech curl, and it drops to the ground. One down, she says, striving to sound cheerful. Three to go.

Although the sun is hot, Marlea continues to shiver. Can you get the one on my arm next?

Percy removes that one and one more. As each one drops, she kicks it down the bank toward the river. She squats for the last one, attached to the inside of Marlea's ankle, and taps her shin. Can you spread a bit?

Marlea widens the space between her feet and stands with hands on hips. That's the last one, right?

Yup. Then you can go back in.

I'm *never* going back in.

With the crisis nearly over, Percy laughs up at Marlea. Until next time.

No. Never. Marlea is relaxed enough to laugh a little herself.

When the last leech curls around the match and drops, Percy flicks it aside. You're bleeding a bit, she says, and wipes the blood with her finger. She glances up quickly, afraid that Marlea might choose this moment to faint, and her eyes are drawn to a bit of pubic hair. She means to stifle her gasp, but Marlea hears.

What?

I hate to say it, but I think there's another one.

Where? Just get it, Marlea says.

Percy, her eyes still on the leech, holds Marlea's leg to steady herself. I think there's one sticking out of your bathing suit. But if you spread your legs again, it'll be all right.

Oh ... Percy ...

It's halfway under your suit.

Marlea is crying. In my crotch?

Percy stands and rubs Marlea's arms. C'mon, don't cry. I can get it. It might even fall off when you get out of your suit.

She slides the straps of Marlea's swimsuit past her shoulders and tugs on the wet elastic. At the sight of Marlea's naked breasts, she steps back. Can't you at least help me?

Marlea bends to peel the wet suit off her body and straightens, adjusting her stance so her legs are spread. She wraps her arms around her breasts. Is it gone?

Percy's fingers tremble. She pulls, a little too roughly, on the flesh of Marlea's upper thigh. No, she says. It's still there. She aims for a look of nonchalance, but she knows she has failed. You're going to have to move your legs farther apart. I don't want to burn you.

Is it in my crotch?

Goddammit. I already said it's in your crotch. She refuses to look at Marlea, just stares single-mindedly at the recalcitrant leech until she stands and retrieves Marlea's towel. Here. It'll be easier if you lie down and put your knees up, like at the doctor's.

Marlea lies on the ground and does as she is told while Percy kneels and positions herself between Marlea's legs.

Is it still there?

For Christ's sake, Marlea! Percy's cheeks are flushed. She bites on her bottom lip. Just be quiet.

Percy—

Shut up!

Marlea turns her head to one side, her eyes filling with tears again. You don't have to be so mean! D'you think I asked all these bloodsuckers to glom onto me?

Percy ignores her. The blood-engorged leech makes an ugly diagonal welt across Marlea's inner thigh. One end stretches out from between tightly coiled pubic hairs; the other end is firmly attached to what Percy tries to view only as a clinical part—the labia majora of her best friend. Her chest pounds.

Just don't move, she says. She pulls again on Marlea's thigh, stretching the skin taut. She lowers the match and is rewarded with a prolonged sizzle. Both ends lift from Marlea's skin as the leech rolls into a protective ball.

Percy has been holding her breath. She sighs. I'm going to try to grab this one and lift it off, otherwise it might roll down and get stuck to you again. She uses the matchbook to pinch the leech between the cover and the remaining matches. Little fucker, she says, throwing the matchbook toward the river. An involuntary shudder runs through her body. I hope there aren't any more.

Make sure, Marlea pleads. She opens her legs as wide as she can. She pulls her knees toward her chest and rolls back on her spine, exposing as much of herself as possible. Am I okay?

Percy feels faint, uncertain whether it is the sight of Marlea so fully exposed or the relief of having successfully rid her of the ugly black bloodsuckers that causes her light-headedness. Nevertheless, she puts one palm on each of Marlea's thighs and examines her vulva carefully. A bruise and a few drops of blood pinpoint the spot where the leech clung. There are no others, but anger she doesn't understand weighs down on Percy's hands. She pushes hard, feeling as if she could separate Marlea's legs from her torso with a quick snap.

Ow. That hurts. Marlea tries to roll forward, to pull her legs together, but Percy continues to push.

Marlea's voice rises. Percy ... let go.

The flush in Percy's cheeks spreads down her neck in blotches. You told me to look. I'm looking.

You're scaring me. Let go.

Percy pushes hard again, then pulls Marlea's legs back into a more comfortable and dignified position. She glares at her. I'm still checking.

Marlea stares back for several seconds. When Percy refuses to break the deadlock, she closes her eyes and adjusts her legs, ankles together on the towel, knees wide apart, almost touching the ground.

Until now, Percy has only seen the outside of Marlea's body—her breasts, the sleek line of leg rounding into buttock, bellybutton a shallow dimple in the long curve up from pubic hair. She has never imagined Marlea like this: rumpled labia, vagina open, insides bright, fading into dark.

Three

PERCY wakes to the acrid odour of smoke and stumbles through her morning weather ritual knowing she'll have the early part of the day, at least, on the ground. Normal visibility is forty kilometres in all directions, although often she can see much farther. Today, as she peers down the trail leading to the airstrip, she guesses she can see one kilometre at best. A quick run partway up the tower ladder confirms this estimate. Visibility: point five kilometres in smoke that has obscured all but the nearest trees.

The radio operator laughs when Percy asks if all the smoke is coming from the fire she spotted yesterday. Not a chance, she says. They're almost ready to put an extinguished on your little fire. This lot drifted in from Saskatchewan overnight. Sure is thick, isn't it?

Yes, and thank Christ it is, Percy thinks. Already she is eager for a break from the long hours in the tower, and poor visibility is a valid excuse. At least I'll have a chance to cut my lawn, she says. Over.

Well, enjoy yourself. I don't imagine you'll be the only one. XMB four-five clear.

Percy sits on the wooden doorstep, legs splayed wide, clad only in a T-shirt and panties, slowly spooning back cereal and milk. Despite the doldrums of last evening, caused by the inevitable letdown following her smoke report and a few imprecise emotional rumblings she represses now, she feels relaxed and buoyantly optimistic. The painted wood is warm beneath her butt, and sounds have taken on a muffled quality, as if everything has been wrapped in cotton batting for the day. Only ants and a few bewildered bluebottles share her immediate space, so that although she might ordinarily feel lonely and restless, instead she feels cocooned and anonymous, somehow suspended in a nebulous chalk-wash of time.

Although she would have trouble articulating why, she knows that this soft-focus view is exactly what she needs just now, and she plans to take her time puttering through the day. If she feels up to reading Marlea's letters, she'll look at them later. She'll cut the grass—that's first on her list—and maybe wash her windows, and she'll simply sit, as she is now, safe and content in a veiled world.

She sets her bowl aside and leans back on her elbows. Over to the east, smoke glows pinkish brown, so she angles her body into the sun's diminished rays and lifts her T-shirt until it is bunched just below her neck. A lusty curve has developed at her waist, and she smiles to see it. She loosens her grip on the T-shirt and watches as the fabric slides to her breasts and catches. When she wriggles a bit, her body is snatched from view. She lifts the shirt up again, over her breasts, then lets it fall once more, relishing the sensation of warm, worn cotton as it glides over hungry skin.

Her rubber boots sit, perfectly aligned, by the door. Although the grass is short, dew this early in the season is heavy, good breeding ground for mosquitoes, and even if she waits until the grass dries, she will need the boots when she mows. The clearing around her cabin is green, strikingly green, and she's required to keep it trim. A previous occupant left a *Non Sequitur* comic strip taped to Percy's refrigerator door. The strip shows the sun relentless in the sky, while a horned devil stands behind some poor clod with a lawn mower. The devil opens his arms in an expansive gesture as if to say: Here it is! And the one with the mower looks out over an endless field of grass. The caption reads:

The Most Plausible Conception of Hell. Pencilled in are the fire tower and Envy River sign.

When Percy first landed at Envy River Tower, she estimated the size of her clearing at three acres. She gaped when the ranger shook his head and corrected her.

More like seven or eight, he said.

And I have to cut it all? With a regular lawn mower?

Only if you want to keep the bugs down, he said.

Percy prefers patios. She prefers interlocking brick with electric bug zappers and benches strategically placed near beds of low maintenance flowers and shrubs. But Envy River Tower is not the city, and she has learned that pushing the lawn mower offers its own rewards. In addition to the sense of accomplishment she feels as each neat swathe lines up against the next, she can almost believe that her hips will melt perfectly, one drop at a time, as she drips in the summer heat.

An hour and a half later, when she actually gets around to cutting the grass, it has not, in fact, dried. Percy has let it grow too long, and the pale stalks remain damp under tenacious seven-inch blades. Every few minutes the mulching vent of the lawn mower—out of which grass normally flies with alarming speed—plugs solid, forcing the mower to stall.

If she didn't have to restart the machine each time, the job would go considerably faster, and so she finds a three-foot length of twine in the shed and uses it to tie the safety bar of the mower to its handle. Now when she releases the handle to unplug the vent, the safety bar remains joined to the handle, and the mower stays running. Although she must still stop every few minutes, gingerly pulling clogged grass from the vent, at least she does not have to wrench her arm from its socket pulling on the stiff cord.

She should do as she used to and schedule an hour of lawn mowing each day. She forgets why she ever stopped the practice, but it worked well. By the end of each week, the entire clearing was cut, and she had only to start over again at the beginning, an endless series of squared off rings tightening into an oblong patch in the middle. But now she remembers why she stopped. The monotony. Every day, round and round. Even for an hour. No thanks.

When the mower plugs again, she checks the time before reaching her gloved hand into the vent. This is taking far too long.

Just chill out, she reminds herself. After all, it takes fewer muscles to smile than to frown.

But the smile she attempts at her own platitude is lost to horrible pain as the end of each leather-covered finger feels as if it has suddenly been blown off. Involuntarily, she drops to the ground, her left hand clamped to her other wrist. As a result of the blade colliding with her fingers, the lawn mower stalls and she is afraid to look. Can't look, in any case, as black splotches float in front of her eyes and obliterate the smoky haze of a moment before.

Oh God, oh God, oh God, she moans. She rolls onto her back, rocks on her spine, still clutching her wrist. Then she rolls onto her side and grinds her open mouth into the soil beneath the damp grass. Her sounds are muffled by the sticky clumps of dirt and grass that she has ground, unaware, past her teeth. She can't breathe. Can't breathe until she finally spits and gasps for air. Then she slobbers into the dirt, still moaning and rocking. She can't stay here. She'll bleed to death. But she needs the ends of her fingers. She can't leave them. She's got to find them. If only she could see.

A moment later, she regains consciousness. She knows

she's been unconscious because it takes some time to recognize the blank, obscured sky swirling to a slow stop above her. She is dizzy, lying on her back with her arm as heavy as concrete at her side. Her left hand has released its grip, and there is no pain, only her dead, useless fingers and nausea swelling, threatening. She knows she must be in shock, and uses her left arm to pull her right hand where she can finally see it. She gasps. The seams at the ends of the first three fingers have burst, and a clean slice-line stands out against the soiled leather, but the tips are not gone. Her fingers must be inside. Her grip on consciousness is tenuous at best, and another wave of nausea nearly flattens her. She has to make her way to the cabin before she passes out again. Carrying her arm, holding it raised and tight to her chest, she staggers and stumbles across the clearing. Her eyesight blotches over again, and twice her legs give way, forcing her to her knees, but each time she rolls back onto her feet. She must get to the radio. She must call for help.

I must, Percy repeats to herself as she staggers through her cabin door. But that is as far as she gets before she collapses completely. She feels her head hit the floor with a solid crack, and then once again she is staring upward in a disoriented fuzz as the room spins into focus.

WHEN Percy regains consciousness for the second time and checks her watch, it is eleven-fifty. More than half an hour has passed since she caught her hand in the blade of the lawn mower. She struggles to a sitting position. Something in the back of her head rolls forward to slam into the top of her skull, wedging there. She closes her eyes and presses her forehead with her good hand. Although she no longer feels as if she will black out at any second, her head now pounds to the angry beat throbbing below her right wrist.

Someone is speaking on the radio, and she strains to hear, worrying that she has missed her call sign while she was unconscious. She sits very still and concentrates. Her ranger is speaking to the duty officer.

That's copied, Jake. The fire is officially extinguished at this time, and we're putting an E on it at one-one-five-zero. Good work.

Percy stops listening. She doesn't bother to get up off the dirty carpet, just sits hunched over her aching hand, hoping she will not faint again. Her fingers feel wet, and she's sure they're sticky. With her teeth, she tugs her left glove free. Now she can get to work on the damaged right. Pinching the split seam at the tip of one gloved finger, she tugs gently. This hurts, but she perseveres. Tug by tug, she frees her hand.

There is swelling and dark, viscous blood. For a second she feels queasy all over again, but she looks away and takes a few deep breaths. Cautiously, with her left hand, she squeezes the fingers of the now empty glove. Nothing. She bows her head and gives herself over to the pounding.

However foolish she was to stick her hand in the mower, she has this, at least, to be thankful for: she has not severed her fingers.

Percy cannot tell whether she needs stitches without washing her hand, so she wobbles to her feet, keeping her right arm close to her chest. She finds peroxide in the bedroom and dumps half a bottle in a small glass bowl. First she dunks her hand in water, swishing slowly until the water turns pink, then in the bowl of peroxide. It is all she can do to remain upright, and as the peroxide changes colour like the water, she breaks out in a cold sweat. She cannot faint. She must know the extent of the damage to her fingers.

She grits her teeth at the terrible sting, grabs a clean towel, and spreads it on the counter. She places her hand on the terry cloth and dabs at her wet fingers with the free end of the towel. The lightest touch causes excruciating pain. Two of her fingers—the index and the middle—are already bruised, and she can see a deep cut on the side of her index finger. Both fingernails are ripped to the quick. Half of one nail is missing, and that part of her finger now looks meaty and bloody. The remaining pieces of nail appear improperly attached. She might pull them free if she tried, but she will bandage them instead. Let them fall off in their own time. Despite her pain, she knows she is fortunate.

The blood appears to be coming from her nail beds, more than from the cut on her index finger, and she can see no need for stitches. If only she can stand the pain, she will bandage herself and manage. She won't be able to wash the windows today, or climb the tower, but no one will have to know.

Percy retrieves her first-aid kit from below her desk. When she has bandaged the cut, doused her fingers in

Mercurochrome, and protected them with a splint, she follows the instructions in the tiny first-aid booklet and fashions a reasonable sling. She tosses back three Tylenol and rushes to collect her afternoon weather. She has ten minutes before the weather call comes through on the radio.

Writing will be awkward for a few days, and she still doesn't know what she will do about climbing the tower, but she will either find a way to do her job, or she will fake it. She has to. The alternative is to admit to the accident and be removed from her tower.

If she had hurt herself any other way, Percy wouldn't hesitate to ask for assistance, but not for this. She will risk missing a fire if it means not having to tell anyone she was stupid enough to shove her hand into the path of a lawn mower blade.

Well. Perhaps she won't risk missing a fire, but she certainly does hope that all this smoke will continue to obscure the surrounding area while she has a chance to heal.

The Tylenol soon takes effect, and all afternoon Percy dozes fitfully, only waking completely when the medication wears off. At night, she soaks her hand in peroxide again, and to quiet the throbbing, which seems worse, she pops three more Tylenol and drinks two screwdrivers. The vodka gets her through the night, but in the morning she is running a fever, and the sky is clear. Her fingers are as black as seaweed and twice their normal size.

XMB four-five, this is XMA six-six-eight.

XMA six-six-eight, this is XMB four-five. Good morning, Percy.

Hi. I know you're just getting ready to take everyone's weather, but I've got a bit of a problem here. I'm running a fever of a hundred and one and there's no way I can get up the tower. Can you get someone to call me? I think I need a doctor. Over.

Of course, Percy. Can I tell them what's wrong? Do you know?

It's an infection, I think.

As soon as she releases the key on her microphone, the ranger cuts in. *XMA six-six-eight, this FH four-one. What's up, Percy?*

Hi, Jake. I ... uh ... hit my hand between a rock and a hard place and it looks infected. It's too swollen to use and I'm dizzy and fevered. An antibiotic and some painkillers would help.

What do you mean a rock and a hard place?

Percy sighs. She knows there are several sets of ears listening. She is shivering and wants only to go back to bed. Even the act of taking a deep breath hurts, and her voice is weak.

I bashed it with a rock, and now it's hurt. And I'm really not doing too well here. I've got to get back to bed.

Okay, Percy. Set your radio to channel twelve and go back to bed. We're going to fly in a replacement and get you to a doctor. Can you get some things ready?

Affirmative. Over.

Okay, don't worry, we'll get there as soon as we can, but I'll call you back on twelve. Can you manage?

Yes. That's affirmative. Thank you. Six-six-eight clear.

Clear to you. MCJ, are you by?

This is MCJ. I copied that, Jake. Should I get warmed up?

Affirmative. You and your machine are on standby as of right now. I'll get back to you in five.

That's copied. MCJ clear.

Percy feels as if she will topple at any second. She switches her radio to channel twelve and lowers her head between her knees. It takes a minute for the queasiness to pass, but she is able to make her way back to bed. She's got an hour to wait, she guesses. Maybe longer if they can't immediately find a spare tower person.

They'll try Gord first, if he's not already working on another tower. He has worked towers for fifteen years or more. For the last three, he's been a spare, filling in because of illness or accidents, or when any tower person requests days off. Those requests are uncommon, but occasionally someone needs to attend a family wedding, or a funeral. Most of the time, the reason is simpler: *Get me out of here before I lose it.*

Percy has felt that way herself often enough, but in seven years she has never asked for a day off. Her take-home pay is about ninety dollars a day. With the season as short as it is, she has always wanted the money more than the freedom, and she has learned to cope. This time, it's not the pay that concerns her. She'll get sick leave—that is the union rule—but she'll lose face as well.

If Gord is unavailable, the pilot will either fly in a member of the initial attack crew—the first crew on a fire—or one of the rangers will stay at her tower temporarily until other arrangements can be made. Percy hopes they'll bring Gord. He's used to taking over on short notice, and he's known for his unobtrusiveness. When he leaves, she will hardly know he was here.

ALMOST three hours pass before they arrive. Jake and the pilot, and Gord with a box of groceries and a backpack; his sleeping gear is rolled into a neat bundle at the top of the pack.

How are you? he asks. He puts his packages on the floor, against the wall and out of the way.

Percy shakes hands awkwardly with her left. I've been better, but I'm all right. Make yourself at home.

Gord sits in a chair at the table and looks around. Nice, he says.

Thanks. Pretty much like all the rest, I guess.

Jake and Gord exchange looks and a laugh. You'd be surprised, Jake says. I wouldn't want to stay at a lot of them.

Dirty?

Gord nods. Worse. Disgusting, some of them. But others are done up real nice. Saunas and everything. One gal made a sweat house out of logs she cut and dragged out of the forest herself.

Percy raises her eyebrows and points to the heavy logs split and built into a picnic table outside her window. Those were here when I came, but they're a nice touch.

They're great. They're not going anywhere.

No. The table weighs a ton. I don't know how they ever dragged the logs here.

There is a pause while everyone stares at the table, then Percy reaches for her jacket. Do you need any last minute orientation or anything?

No. I'll find what I need. Gord points at her hand, still in the sling. I hope you're okay.

Thanks. I'll be okay once I get to a doctor.

So what exactly happened? Jake asks. I wasn't too clear on what you meant. You hit it with a rock?

Percy hooks her bag over her shoulder and acts as if she has heard nothing. She looks at the others expectantly. I'm ready, she says.

Jake points to Percy's bandaged hand. We're going to have to fill out some paperwork and get all the details on that.

Percy nods. There's not much to tell, but I need to see the doctor first, if that's okay. Her face is flushed and her eyes shiny.

I hear you. He turns to Gord. Okay, buddy, you're on your own.

Percy raises her hand in a wave and heads out the door. She is in the air before she remembers she meant to bring the letters from Marlea.

THE helicopter transports Percy to High Level, where she is given an intravenous drip and confined to the hospital that first night, and for a second as well, until her temperature drops back to normal.

She admits to her stupidity and responds firmly when Jake begins to lecture. I know, she says. I've learned my lesson, and I'm sure I'll never hear the end of it. Let's just fill out the damn forms. Then she relents. Can we *please* keep this quiet?

I don't know how, Percy. The secretary has to type up the report. The chief has to see it. Jake grins and shakes his head. Don't worry. Nobody will laugh at you to your face. It's only behind your back that they'll say you're an idiot.

Surely I'm not the first idiot—

You are.

Well. There's nothing she can do but pretend nonchalance. *Well,* she says again. I guess I am then.

The doctor stitches the cut, removes both fingernails, and dresses her fingers loosely, protecting them from bumps with an aluminum splint. He confirms that no bones are fractured, and assures Percy that she can remove the splint as soon as the nail beds toughen up. Although the skin will remain bruised for weeks, the swelling is nearly gone by the time she leaves the hospital.

No one wants her climbing the tower while she's taking medication containing codeine, so she settles into the bunkhouse at the ranger station for a further three days. Except for taking long, luxurious showers under a real showerhead, there is little to do except watch satellite television and go for walks down the dusty road. From Percy's perspective, this is just as well. Inhabiting a peopled world requires skills she has temporarily lost.

She is accustomed to the disorientation that accompanies the end of the tower season, but her inability to bridge the two worlds now—after little more than a month alone—leaves her feeling cross and disconcerted. In her imagination, she is another person, capable and bright, one people count on in moments of confusion. Here, she goes mute if more than one person at a time speaks to her.

When she drives to the grocery store in search of snack food, she clenches the steering wheel with sweaty palms. Her splints are straight and rigid. Her other fingers curl so tightly they ache. She sits trembling at a four-way stop, unsure whether to turn or wait for oncoming traffic, and this in a town so small she nearly misses the signs and drives right past when she first arrives each spring.

More than ever, she craves the comforting familiarity of Marlea's voice, and when she sees a phone booth, she slows to a crawl. She is torn between two conflicting needs—call right now, and never call again. She almost turns in at the booth, but someone behind her honks and, flustered, she drives on.

The IGA is one quarter the size of the neighbourhood Safeway she's accustomed to in Calgary, yet Percy stands in the aisle for ten minutes, staring at candy bars, popcorn, potato chips, licorice. Finally, overwhelmed, she flees the bright lights, the other shoppers, and makes her way empty-handed back to the ranger station. Alone in her tiny room, she sits on the narrow single bed and breathes deeply. I'm okay, I'm okay, I'm okay, she says.

At the tower, she has a routine. Everything happens sequentially, one task at a time, in any order she decides. The simplicity soothes her, and she needs it now.

After five days away, she asks to return, and she is flown back. Sore fingers or not, she is better off at her tower. Except for Marlea, her life is fine just the way it is.

Still, Gord has hardly lifted off in the helicopter before Percy goes to the drawer for Marlea's letters. She can harldy believe that only a week has passed since she threw them there following her last tower service. So much has happened, and Marlea knows none of it.

She sits perched on the outside step weighing the letters—two of them—in her hand. She checks the postmarks and deliberates over which one she should open first. A woodpecker hammers in the distance, and flies buzz incessantly. An ant crosses the step beside her foot and disappears. She turns the letters over and over, wanting to open them but not wanting to as well.

Without reading them, she is certain she knows the tone—I miss you *but*. You have a problem. You're angry. I, on the other hand, am managing friendliness as usual, am thinking of you with love despite everything. Blah, blah, blah.

She doesn't always know how to respond to these chatty little messages from Marlea, vignettes of day-to-day life with Andrew, and this year she's not certain she can respond at all. Marlea's polite, controlled emotion leaves her with no defence. Yes, she should manage her own anger better. Yes, she should let Marlea live the life she has chosen. And finally, yes: perhaps the time has come to look elsewhere for what she wants and needs.

She stands and kicks a stone. She is tearing herself apart, and there is no one to tell. Not her parents, who would never admit that her closeness to Marlea is anything other than friendship, nor her brother, who has become so distant that he can barely exchange jokes, let alone intimacies. Her friends would listen, of that she's certain, but how many times can one person cry over another and still expect sympathy? She has mentioned nothing to anyone, yet she feels as if she is getting a divorce—from someone who has never committed to her. She hates the way she thinks in terms of marriage and divorce too. What if she and Marlea *had* agreed to spend their lives together? She doesn't mind leaving the religious ceremony to those who believe it's important, but shouldn't the public registry, at least, be open to everyone?

She picks another rock from the ground and aims at a tree. The rock strikes dead on. She hides her face in her hands.

When she's had her moment of self-pity, she stuffs the unopened letters into the garbage pail, hides them under banana peels and a large black mound of Gord's soggy coffee grounds.

So this is it then. She has chosen to move on, the way Marlea has always chosen—yet this choice feels like no choice at all, merely resignation. She'd like to make Marlea breakfast as Andrew does, pour more coffee or tease her out of morning moodiness, but she wants to do this honestly, as her lover, as her life partner, not in the sleazy, frightened way Marlea (or worse yet, Andrew) occasionally allows.

Just thinking about the way Marlea applauds Andrew's acceptance of her infidelity makes Percy fume. How doting would he be if Percy were a man? Considerably less, she thinks. A man might pose a real threat.

I can't believe you told him we used a dildo, Percy said only last fall. She rolled toward the wall, shook Marlea off.

He asked, that's all, said Marlea. I didn't think you'd care.

Of course I care. To him a dildo is still, and always will be, a substitute penis, something less, not just an occasional toy. Besides, you and I don't talk about your sex life with Andrew. I don't want to talk about it. And I don't think he should know anything about us. It's none of his—

I don't know—

Jesus Christ, Marlea! You think he looks at a dildo and doesn't think penis? Give me a break. It's probably never entered his head that you can have sex without a cock. What would we *do*, for God's sake?

Percy knows too that if she could up the ante financially, Andrew would not be so confident. The logic of lack, she thinks. No penis, no money, no power. Even her identity is ambiguous, neither heterosexual nor homosexual. Yet she doesn't feel as if she is half and half—half cream and half milk, merely waiting to see which part will rise to the top. Lesbians know. Straight people know. If bisexuals know, then she's not that either.

MARLEA and Andrew met in cooking school the year Percy and Marlea turned twenty-three. At first they were friends. After that, lovers. By the end of the second year, Andrew had moved into Marlea's apartment.

You can't let him move in! Percy said. You must be joking.

Marlea, standing quiet and determined, was not joking.

In a moment of frightened panic, a sudden surge of bleakness, Percy smashed her hand through a glass pane. She pulled her hand back to examine it, first the back, then the palm, as well as her arm. Not a scratch.

Maybe you're invincible, Marlea said. She looked at Percy's French doors and turned to smash her own fist through a corresponding pane of glass.

Blood streamed from her knuckles and ran down into the crisp cotton cuff of her white, white shirt. Cold winter air streamed into the room, and Marlea broke out in a sweat. She tried a smile, then shrugged and lowered herself to the carpet.

Marlea needed Percy, and Percy responded by becoming quietly efficient. She wrapped Marlea's hand in a towel, drove through snow to the hospital, and spent three hours waiting with her in the emergency room.

This is all my fault, Percy said. I'm sorry, so sorry. You should do whatever you need to do. I love you. I will always be your friend. Always.

Then Andrew arrived. He dismissed Percy with a quick nod and sat in a chair opposite Marlea. Tenderly, he unwound Percy's towel from around Marlea's fist. His face blanched at the sight of so much blood.

Can't we get a goddamn doctor here? he yelled, then waved Marlea's protests aside and stalked up to the admitting desk. We've got someone *bleeding* over there, he said, pointing at Marlea.

Percy squeezed Marlea's shoulder and made her way past several other patients who had been waiting just as long or longer than she and Marlea had. She fastened her fingers around Andrew's arm and moved toward the door.

What? Andrew said. I was only trying to get some goddamn help.

They exited the building and hunched and shivered in the cold.

What you need to realize is that we've been here for three hours. You can't just walk in and snap your fingers.

Andrew shot Percy a hostile look. D'you want to tell me what happened? I find it hard to believe that Marlea punched a window on her own account.

Percy wished it was Andrew sitting inside bleeding. She looked at his thin concerned face, at his trendy hair and trendy clothes, at the slight curl of his lip as he spoke, and she knew that he was unworthy of Marlea.

You're right, she said. I took Marlea's fist and punched it through the window myself, you asshole.

I didn't mean that. It's just not Marlea's style. She doesn't go around punching things.

No, she doesn't. It's my fault. I thought I saw your face in the glass and I punched it. Then she copied me.

Look. I don't know what your problem is—

Oh, sure! Like you didn't think I'd be upset if you and Marlea moved in together? I can't stand you.

What is your problem? We've been living together for over a month! Why didn't you get all bent out of shape when we did it? What's so special about today?

Percy reached out a hand to steady herself against the brick wall. What do you mean? You've been living at Marlea's for a month?

Andrew looked confused. I've been there since before Christmas. You mean you didn't know?

Percy shook her head. No. I didn't know. She just told me tonight. That you *were* moving in. Not that you already had. Percy put her hands over her face and leaned against the wall.

Andrew reached out and touched her shoulder. Hey. Are you all right?

Percy shook him off. No. I'm not all right. I'm getting out of here.

She didn't move. How could Marlea have lied to her— and for all these weeks? Percy took her hands from her face and confronted Andrew. You do know that we're lovers? That Marlea likes women?

Andrew sighed and twisted his lips into a wry smile. Yes. I know that you're lovers. And that you're very important to her, when you're not off experimenting with everybody else.

Why don't you go fuck yourself, she said, but she took no pleasure in it. And I'm not just *important* to her, she *loves* me.

Andrew made his tone more conciliatory. She's not a lesbian, and she wants to be with *me*. She loves me too.

Percy shook her head. Most people say I'm not a lesbian either. But that doesn't change anything. All I know is that I love her, and she loves me. You'll see.

We've already talked about it. I don't own her. Maybe she'll want to be with a woman sometimes. I'm okay with that.

Well, aren't you a big-hearted prick.

Look, I'm getting tired of this. Andrew blew on his hands to warm them, then shoved them deep in his pockets. I should thank you. We probably wouldn't be living together at all if you hadn't started going out with Dwayne.

The way Andrew said *Dwayne*, as if Dwayne was the biggest dork alive, infuriated Percy. Never mind that she agreed.

I asked her to live with me before, Andrew said, to marry me even, but she always said no, she wasn't ready. And then you wouldn't even return her calls.

Like she cared.

She did care, but all you cared about was getting even because she was spending too much time with me.

Percy knew there was truth in what he said. Oh, fuck off. The last thing I need is *you* analyzing *me*. She pulled her collar up and ducked her head inside its warmth. I'll tell you what, you just tell Marlea I'll check on her later. Maybe.

See? That's what you do. She needs you, and you walk away every time—

Percy whirled around. Just fuck off, would you? And don't think she won't lie to you, too.

That night it was forty below zero, sixty with a wind chill, and Percy heard her mother's voice, as unrelenting as the wind—*You'll never love anyone but yourself. You don't know how to love.* And Marlea's voice—*I told him he could move in.*

Percy had purposely ignored Marlea. She spent Christmas in San Francisco, and then almost every night at Dwayne's apartment until recently. She had erased Marlea's telephone messages without returning them, and had lied and said she was busy when she sat at home alone.

Sometimes, in her confusion, Percy didn't know what to think. But that night she knew Marlea was right. Of course she was unreasonable. Happiness eluded her, and in trying to wound Marlea, she had ruined everything. While she attempted to secure the future, she destroyed the present. Like her mother, she realized, she had a talent for unhappiness, a congenital flaw for which there was no cure.

Idiot, she said to herself. You're an idiot and a bully. But the words emptied into emptiness, and deliberately Percy uncovered the broken panes on her balcony doors.

For an hour she lay naked under a sheet on the couch. Frost replaced any heat that hung in the air, and as her body began to shake, she held her limbs still and straight—wouldn't allow herself to curl into her own warmth. She watched Johnny Carson without hearing a word, and when her teeth chattered, she was pleased, but still afraid that drowsiness would not come soon enough.

She had called Marlea earlier in the evening, not to discuss anything, but only to check that Marlea was all right. Even then, her plan was in place. She complained that her apartment was cold, and then left the television on so it would look as if she had naturally fallen asleep on the couch. She took no alcohol or pills, left no note, but she should have at least drunk herself into a stupor and made the cold easier to bear. She wrapped the sheet tighter and prayed for sleep. Please God, let me sleep, let me sleep.

But what kind of god would answer a prayer like that? Of course Marlea was right. Percy could think only of herself. And what about her parents and Bobby? Wouldn't they miss her, or worse, blame themselves? Wouldn't Marlea wonder forever if there was something she could have done differently? Maybe even Andrew? And what would they inscribe on her tombstone? *Here lies someone who, in all the world, could find nothing for which to stay alive?* What a legacy. What arrogance and impatience.

The cold burned her skin. Despite herself, she curled around her aching belly, the only heat left there like fire. She could think of nothing but the cold, and although she wanted not to, she sought warmth in the bones of her ankles where she grasped them. Her fingers were numb; her cheeks felt hard. She shouldn't. And what's more, she couldn't. God forgive her, she still wanted to die, but she couldn't. She hadn't the strength. She was a bully, and a coward too.

PERCY and Marlea didn't argue often, but when they did, Andrew was almost always the cause.

You're just using me, Percy said, the evening before she left for the tower. You don't give a shit about me. She spoke matter-of-factly, had gone beyond anger to some still place inside herself where hurt and distrust had flattened into disappointment so deep it resembled calm.

I'm not using you. And I do give a shit.

Marlea had recently turned thirty, and she was more beautiful than ever. For the past five years she had lived with Andrew and had often fallen into bed with Percy.

On this last night together, Percy was moved less by Marlea's beauty than by her wounded expression—as if she was the one who had wanted commitment and had received only watered-down sharing.

Percy cried, made herself vulnerable once more, while Marlea lay still and pale on the other side of some invisible line that split the bed into two awful, unrelated halves.

You seduced *me*, Marlea said. Although her body was undeniably lithe and strong like a dancer's, with well-defined muscles running the length of it, she somehow appeared frail and limp in Percy's bed. I don't want to hurt you, but you're the one who started this whole thing. I can't just dump Andrew. He's not a high school crush, and he doesn't ask me to be any different. You're the only one who insists on more.

Oh *right*. I seduced you and I've been forcing myself on you ever since! Get to know yourself! And Andrew doesn't have to insist. What does he lack besides a bit of time with you—time he seems just as happy to spend out golfing with his buddies?

Marlea's body came to life. She no longer looked frail and weak, an exhausted victim, but was spring-loaded, ready to fight or flee. Her voice and eyes sliced through Percy. *Andrew is the one who should be angry.*

But of course he isn't, said Percy. He's always understanding and perfect, in his own Milquetoast way.

Marlea clutched the sheet to her body and struggled out of bed. *Don't say another word. You've said enough. I've had it.*

Percy sat up. *You've* had it? She motioned to the pile of clothes Marlea streched for, her voice incredulous. You've had it, and now you're going back to Andrew? On the mention of his name, her voice rose, her palm slammed into the wall. Go, then. Back to home base. *I've* had it.

Percy felt her own transformation into someone cool and stiff. Fire vixen or ice queen, Marlea had said often enough—either hot or cold—but Percy saw herself differently. When she could, she communicated honestly, sometimes diplomatically, sometimes not. And she was working on eliminating the *not*. Other times, she used all her energy to keep herself quiet. She was afraid that if she didn't hold on tight, keep her mouth shut, she might let go and start smashing things. Not outside objects like the collectibles or artwork Marlea had given her over the years. No. She felt as if her own body was glass in danger of breaking. She might snap one index finger at the knuckle. Here, Marlea, have a bauble. Might slap her other palm against the wall and watch the hand shatter. She could whack her head, a big glass globe, on the window casing to create an impressive spectacle, eyeballs under the bed, glass shards stuck in carpet, in curtains. Watch out for the glass—Percy lost her head today.

So she held her voice steady, matter-of-fact again. I'm going to the tower tomorrow and when I come back, I never want to see you again. I'm finished.

From the outside she looked cold and unfeeling. Inside, desire had lodged so deeply in her body she was afraid it might never surface again.

WHEN the alarm buzzes at seven-fifteen, Percy taps the clock into silence and lets her eyes fall shut again. She doesn't want to wake. In her dreams, life is decided, either nightmarish or not, and she wishes she could stay suspended there. The trouble with waking is that the facts of her life remain as complicated as ever.

But the space between conscious and unconscious narrows, and Percy knows that if she dares to lie still for even a minute more, she won't wake until the sound of other towers passing morning weather alerts her to the fact that she is too late to gather her own.

She kicks aside covers and flails at the mosquito net, batting at the spot where the opening should be, cursing the manufacturer who might have thought to make an escape visible. Both the floor and the air are cold when she finally locates an edge to the netting and slides her legs out over the side of the bed. She forces herself to her feet and reaches out to grope for the chair that holds clothes of the day before. The room is bright with early morning sun, but her eyelids object.

Her mother once told her that rising early would get easier as she got older, and she wonders now how many more years must pass before she admits to herself that rising will never get easier. Every night, when she considers setting the alarm to go off five or ten minutes earlier so she won't need to rush, she decides that the extra minutes of sleep in the morning are crucial, will somehow help her to wake more easily, although they never have.

She bends close to peer at the clock. Seven-twenty. She

hitches yesterday's jeans and zips. Dancing and stumbling, she finally gets her feet in socks before she forces her eyes to adjust to the light and checks the mirror on the wall. Her hair is heavy, wild, a mess of troublesome red curls. With her eyes half closed, she looks like a stick on fire. A matchstick. She wishes she could burn out and never have to work or think again.

Instead, in her boots and a warm jacket, Percy steps outside into the morning dazzle. At the ladder, she grabs a rung and moves as quickly as she can. No dawdling up the tower this morning. Her hands are leather-gloved to protect her palms against the bite of angle iron, yet even with gloves her right hand still hurts where the lawn mower cut it. One hundred rungs. One hundred feet. At the top of the ladder she pushes the trap door open above her head and drags herself into the cupola, checking the sky, observing washboard ripples of high light cloud. She divides the sky into tenths. Six parts clouded, four parts so blue she feels as if she could slam right into it.

She pulls her notebook from a pocket and scribbles. June 5. Two parts high cloud, three parts middle, one part cumulus. High two, middle three, CU one. She scans the horizon and jots in the notebook again. Visibility: twenty-five kilometres in haze. She checks the time, wants to omit the smoke observation, but there's no point. If she neglects her duties now, she'll feel guilty and anxious later, will have to make an extra trip up only to reassure herself that the whole forest isn't on fire.

Maybe she can skip the ten o'clock check, she thinks, knowing she can't, and forces herself to slow down, to survey the whole 360 degrees of protected area with binoculars held steady. No smoke, and so back down the ladder. Seven-forty.

The first call comes through on the outside speaker as she checks the rain gauge.

All stations, this is XMA four-five by for the morning weather. Go ahead seven-four-six.

Percy scribbles. Only one point four millimetres of rain—a shower yesterday afternoon, but not nearly enough to make a difference in her rain barrel. Her boots are shiny and wet with dew, and she kicks through the grass on her way to the Stevenson screen. The door of the screen is latched at head height; she unhooks it and peers inside. Maximum temperature yesterday: eight. Minimum temperature: three. She flips a switch to set the fan going and closes the door so air will circulate unhindered as the forced breeze passes through slatted wood and cools a strip of moistened gauze on a thermometer—the wet bulb. The difference between wet bulb and dry bulb decides humidity.

She tips her head back and stares up. Attached to a pole eighty feet up the tower, anemometer cups spin at high speed; she'll know exactly how fast the wind blows when she checks the electronic read-out inside the cabin. The weather vane points north.

Any idiot could do this, but it is her job. Part of her job. Again, she opens the door to the Stevenson screen. Wet bulb three point five, dry bulb an even four degrees. She half-walks, half-runs to the cabin. Two more stations to report before hers. Inside or out, she hears the same towers every morning.

What a cushy job, friends in the city gush. What do you do all day?

I don't know. I work. Mow the lawn, sand, paint. Do repairs, check equipment, listen for the radio. Watch for smoke fifty hours a day. I read, write letters, carve. I work more hours than I'm paid, but it's all the same. Only thing that changes is the weather.

Must have lots of time to think.

Plenty of time to think.

Inside, Percy checks the anemometer read-out. Wind twenty-three kilometres, gusting forty. This information, along with the rest from her notes, she transfers to another sheet so she can read the figures off in the correct order. From a set of tables, she determines the relative humidity, totals the numbers for dry bulb, wet bulb, wind, and rain, and then writes the figure under Grand Total just as Gilmore begins reciting his weather.

Percy's report follows Gilmore's, and this morning, as he speaks, she reaches for the radio to rest her fingertips lightly on the speaker.

No precip, he says. *Clouds high two, middle one.*

With each phrase, she feels his voice vibrate, his presence course through her hand so that she imagines her fingers light on his throat, his vocal cords oscillating beneath her touch. The radio feels warm, helps to bring the image to life, and she wonders how her vibrations differ from his.

Six-six-eight, this is four-five by for the morning weather.

Four-five, this is six-six-eight.

Percy holds the mike in her right hand as she reports; her left she leaves on the radio. The vibrations are distinctly different. Hers are shorter, quicker. She smiles at the radio as if it were not only talking, but breathing as well.

He has received her e-mail, she is sure, and he knows that she went out to the hospital. At this moment he's listening, wondering about her as she wonders about him.

Now that she has reported her weather, she could return to bed, could think about him there, but the radio will bleep on and off with bits and pieces of forestry command for the rest of the day, possibly well into the evening. Each squawk will interrupt her thoughts, and she will listen just long enough to determine that the message is not for her. She's accustomed to these interruptions and barely notices the way her body remains always on edge, always waiting, waiting, rarely answering.

The kettle needs refilling, so she makes another trip outside for water from the rain barrel. Then, as she waits for the water to heat, she stitches red thread along the opening of the mosquito net, glancing up once in a while, wishing she had more light. Like all forestry cabins, this one is a modest, wall-boarded space, long ago designed to be inexpensively practical rather than attractive. Still, it's a space that appeals to her because she has no need to judge it satisfactory or not. When she arrives, she can't ask to see another room, can't say, I'll think about it, or, Perhaps I'll come back later. Like it or not, this is what she gets for the duration, for every season she chooses to return to Envy River.

A few minutes later, using a corn broom, she works on the worn and defiled carpet. Every year, she asks that this carpet be replaced with linoleum she can sweep and wash clean. Every year she returns to the same reddish-brown layer of indoor/outdoor immovable filth.

She wears shoes all the time, and she would rather stand barefoot outside than inside; even scrubbing with a bristled brush and liquid cleaner has made no difference.

Her friends call this simple living.

Unrefined, she says, but certainly not simple. Everything takes longer at the tower.

When Percy is finished tidying up, for instance, she'd like to walk into the washroom, turn on the taps, adjust the water temperature, and step into the spray of a warm shower. That would be simple. But here, there is no washroom.

Instead, she props her shower-bag in the sink and attempts to pour, without spilling, a kettle of warm water into the narrow opening. Using a funnel would make sense, but she doesn't have one, and although she could improvise—the top half of a plastic bottle, for starters—she somehow always forgets until she finds herself pouring, wishing she had remembered earlier.

She never used to think much about water as a nonrenewable resource, and she knows there are times at home when she has used the equivalent of fifteen or twenty kettles without a thought, but out here, where a full kettle is considered a generous shower, she is cognizant of just how precious water is. When she has finished pouring, she tightens the nozzle on the shower-bag and hangs it on the outside hook.

As the warm water trickles over her head, off her shoulders, and down her torso, Percy feels a surge of pleasure— her first today. Because the morning air is still cool, bugs are not yet out in abundance, and the temptation is strong to let the trickle flow unhindered, to warm her skin and flatten her goose bumps. Instead, she turns the nozzle shut, soaps in the cold air, and rinses briefly. Her breasts strain away from her body, ache for touch. To keep her mind off the cold, she starts at the beginning of the alphabet and imagines that she is an amoeba, body rounding out and hunching up, spreading itself ahead of her cold fingers.

Amoeba, body, cold. ABC. *Don't* want to *end* my shower until *Friday.* G. She's up to the letter G in this game that makes no sense but occupies her mind anyway. She tries Gilmore's name on her tongue—*Gilmore*—then inserts him whole into her fantasy, feels his warm fingers on cold breasts lifting, nipples hard wrinkles tucked into sudsy palms. She likes her breasts, likes the muscles that define the ball of her belly as her hands slide down. H. *Hands* confidently at her waist, slippery over *hips*. Callused hands, she thinks. Big, wet loofah hands sponging up and down her legs, into the small of her back. She widens the space between her thighs until all the flesh of her body arcs around loofah hands ever so careful between her legs.

Two years ago, Marlea flew in with Percy's grocery service and stayed for two weeks. The days passed swiftly, fourteen days of giddy companionship, and every morning, when the sun broke through, they took turns in the shower, watching each other soap and rinse as if they were still school children in the old blue bus. Percy has never tired of seeing Marlea naked, and that summer she wished the water would run endlessly, a warm shower from the sky that would keep them each tilting and turning indefinitely.

You look eighteen, she had told Marlea. No, better than you looked at eighteen. What's that old saying? *Young people are acts of nature. Old people are works of art.* Someday you're going to be one work of art.

After their showers, they'd go up the tower for a while before lunch, squeezing into the hammock together, one in each end, swinging gently, talking and laughing about not much at all. Percy would report the afternoon weather, and then they'd cook—jumbo shrimp with vegetables and lemon on a bed of coconut rice, couscous salad, macaroni and cheese. It didn't matter. They would leave the dishes and play crib and gin rummy, snacking on strawberries and Brie, not because they were hungry, but because Marlea had brought them, and for Percy they were a novelty.

In my tower. H, I, J. *Just* Gilmore and me in my tower.

Playing the *kazoo* and feeling nothing but *l-lust*. *L-l-laugh-ing*. Percy's teeth chatter as she shapes these last words in her mouth.

The fantasies and the game—both must end because she can no longer stand the cold. Her hair holds shampoo like a sponge, but there are only a few cups of warm water left. She slaps a mosquito, its proboscis buried deep in her shoulder, and her own blood splats across the surface of her skin. She flicks the mosquito into the air and rinses. There is hardly enough warm water to wash the suds from her face, let alone her hair.

Her skin looks fresh plucked, is already stretched taut over a proliferation of bumps. She might as well go all the way and freeze her skull as well. She lifts the lid on the rain barrel and scoops a small pot of cold water, bends her neck and dumps the water over her head. Pain shoots through her eyes. She stamps her bare feet, and with icy fingers tests a strand of hair for the telltale squeak. No suds. Close enough.

In the bedroom, Percy shivers and dries, dressing for the second time. Same jeans, fresh underwear, and fresh, although stained, T-shirt. In the heat of the summer, she will remove the arms of the T-shirt, will perhaps cut a V into the neckline or hack the bottom off at midriff length. Except for the clothes in which she arrives and leaves, her entire wardrobe is made up of old, unwanted clothing, duds to do anything in.

There is a certain amount of freedom in this, and she gets filthy sometimes. Sweated-up, grease-stained, paint-splotched, and there isn't a soul to notice or care. If one sock wears out, she matches it with another, to hell with the colours. She likes herself better this way, free of fashion rules she's never quite succeeded at anyway, yet she'd be mortified if anyone saw.

She shakes her tangled hair back and faces the mirror. Nothing changes except the weather and my underwear, she says, grinning into and out from the mirror. Off to one side, tucked in the frame, Marlea grins too, fingers in her mouth pulling her lips into a grotesque jack-o'-lantern smirk, eyes laughing into the camera. Because of Marlea's eyes, Percy moves her photo from home to tower, from tower to home, even now.

SHE logs on daily, sometimes two or three times a day, anticipating Gilmore's reply, and today, when Percy enters her password and is rewarded with *Two new messages for pturner*, she knows intuitively that one of them is from Gilmore. She executes the receive commands twice before her fingers and her mind work in tandem.

His message scrolls by as the transfer is made. She makes no attempt to read it but waits, instead, until the printer slides the page into her hands, a permanent copy of what she hopes are intimate details.

Date: 07 Jun 08:52:06
From: Gilmore A. Graham <gills@agt.net>
To: pturner@direct.ca
Subject: Pleased to meet you

Dear Percy Turner,

I know you've only been back on your tower for a few days, but I wanted to say that I'm sorry you were ill, and that I hope you're doing fine now. I'm happy you copied my address, and by all means, let's get to know each other. Why don't you tell me what you do with yourself when you're not here?

I've heard you on the radio as well. Interesting name, I thought, because I'm sensitive to names. All my life I've been plagued by the ambiguity of mine: Is that Gilmore Graham or Graham Gilmore? And then there's the matter of my middle name: Audrey, if you can believe it. My grandfather's name. I remember the look on my mother's face when I carved my initials

into a pumpkin one fall. I was fourteen, I think. GAG, she said. Her eyes
went wide and she stared at me with such a look. I'll never forget it.

So I'm glad you wrote. I was surprised ... not too many people out here
with e-mail. I notice voices too, and yours is an interesting mix of gentle-
ness and determination. Or so I imagine, Percy Turner.

Percy blinks at the page. That's it? She turns to the screen
and scrolls to the beginning of the message: 1230 bytes,
including the header. She searches for her response, pats
around carefully inside herself, but feels nothing she can
name. This surprises her, as if she has encountered a blank
screen where she expected to find a complicated document.

She reads the message again. An interesting mix of fact
and humour, and she wonders if he took as long composing
this message as she took composing hers. She checks the
header. Gilmore A. Graham. Apparently he's not putting
her on about his initials. And he *does* say she sounds gentle.

Gentle is a quality she'd like to have linked to her name.
She prefers it to the ones she's accustomed to hearing—
independent, strong, diligent, creative. All good solid qualities, she knows, but better in an employee than a lover,
certainly without allure. She supposes one is born into some
adjectives and chooses others; given a choice, she'd elect to
be associated with words like seductive, charming, mysteri-
ous, gracious. Words that allude to flawless skin, and love-
liness, and impeccable taste. Or, if denied those, through
plainness or a tendency toward frankness, she would opt for
ones that denote compassion and caring—tender, kindly,
considerate, magnanimous, and yes, gentle.

The second e-mail message is from Marlea. Percy high-
lights the subject line. Before she can reconsider, she presses
the delete key.

THE sky is low and grey, and a light drizzle has reduced visibility to only a few kilometres, so there is no need to climb the tower. Instead, as she ambles along the trail toward the airstrip, Percy rattles a special walking stick she has designed and carved herself. She knows that bears are normally as eager to avoid her as she is to avoid them, so she has topped the stick with a six-inch length of steel pipe. A few small ball bearings sealed into the pipe cavity clink with each step.

As she walks, she is oblivious to bluebells and daisies lining the trail, and at the airstrip, although she sees hundreds of tiny wild strawberries, each one no bigger than a pencil eraser, ripe and delectably red, she walks without stooping to pick them. She wanders aimlessly, thinking about Gilmore's e-mail and trying to assess her reasons for the initial exchange. She was attracted to his voice and wanted to make contact, it is true, but now that he has responded, what does she really want from him? That she had wanted to take her thoughts off Marlea is clear; where she hopes the exchanges will lead now is something else entirely.

She tells herself that she merely wants conversation, or to gain a friend. Certainly she has no romantic interest in a man she has never met and can only foolishly invent from tidbits of information snatched here and there. Yet she knows that at some level she is lying to herself. To deny how she longs for an immediate fix-all would be to pretend a self-reliance she doesn't feel. In the most guileless part of her mind, she knows this, but rather than admit to what she knows—which would require that she first dig up old ground and lay Marlea to rest with a proper burial—Percy begins to imagine a future that requires no old bones. Out of a low grey sky and light drizzle, she glimpses the after-angst of pleasure yet to be discovered in a man who, for a while at least, can be anything she wishes.

Date: 08 Jun 23:22:45
From: Percy Turner <pturner@direct.ca>
To: gills@agt.net
Subject: Hi again

Gilmore (Do you like to be called Gilmore, or Gil?),

Hi. I'm so glad you wrote back. I hoped you would, and I'm looking forward to chatting with you. You may have noticed that I don't talk on the radio much—too many ears (like mine) listening, but I don't avoid it altogether. As you're new to this district, I should tell you that they don't mind if we talk once in a while, so long as it's in the evening after sked. We usually switch to channel twelve, to pretend we have some privacy and so as not to bother anyone, but as soon as you say, "Meet you on channel twelve," everyone else will switch there as well. Just so you know. I'm sure it's the same everywhere.

I liked your letter. The story about your mother made me laugh out loud. Are you close to her?

As for what I do when I'm not here: well ... although I haven't really succeeded, I try to keep my life in the city as uncomplicated as life here. I carve walking sticks and odd little figures mostly, so when the weather is warm enough, I'm on my balcony in Calgary, overlooking the river, carving. I don't make a bundle, but with what I save from summers here, I get by. Sometimes, as I sit in the sun, peeling a bit of bark down the length of a stick, I wonder how I ever managed to stumble into such a satisfying life. Other times, I run up and down a scale of lethargy that often ends with me huddled under my comforter for days, wondering who would miss me if I never crawled out.

I hope that doesn't strike you as too intimate—my telling you that in my second letter—but I'm feeling a bit sad tonight. The late hour as much as anything, I guess. Or perhaps the rain is getting to me.

June is always a bit tough for me, and every year around this time I suddenly feel very sad, as if I only have a six-week limit on aloneness. For six weeks I feel fine; I settle in, wind down after a winter in the city, get used to the tower again, and then one day, bam—I feel totally alone. I've checked my journals and it's the same every year.

Anyway, enough of that. You ended your letter by saying, "Or so I imagine." Sometimes I imagine so much out here that I wonder if I still know the difference between imagination and memory. Or the present, for that matter. How about you?
Percy

AFTER evening sked—the final radio check with all towers—Percy sits by the radio, hoping Gilmore will choose this night to have a friendly conversation. Not with her, of course, because then she would have to disguise the uneasiness in her voice—the need for him to like her, the need to know more—and she's not confident that she could. She hopes he will call someone else, or that someone will call him, so she can learn more without risking a thing.

Only once in the last two months has she heard him speak sociably. That discussion was with the radio operator, and Percy learned that Gilmore lives in Edmonton, that he used to have a job as a social worker. Now he writes—magazine articles mostly, but he has had modest success with two books of non-fiction. He worked on fire towers when he attended university, and he still likes to fill in occasionally because the isolation provides a solid block of time in which to write.

So how do you keep from going stir-crazy at the tower? Kim asked.

He just laughed. I don't, he said. Writers go stir-crazy anywhere, but I spend a lot of time on the computer researching, talking to people on the Internet, learning new things. News items are good for giving me ideas. But what about you? he said, changing the subject. Why do you spend your summers talking on the radio?

Percy likes that about Gilmore. That he doesn't get caught up talking only about himself the way a lot of people do. He's not evasive; it's only that he knows how to facilitate the gentle swing back and forth between someone else's

ideas and his own, all the time sounding genuinely interested. But it is his responses that she waits to hear. He is a
writer after all, and behind each answer must lie a lifetime
of listening and thought.

She wishes he'd talk more, but what she likes most is his
laughter. When Gilmore is pleased on the radio, he emits a
pleasant rumble from his chest, like that of distant thunder
before one sharp clap of laughter escapes, an extended *hah!*
of surprise and pleasure. A reward, Percy thinks, for anyone
who is able to startle him with humour. Not that *she* has
yet, but she hopes to.

At eleven o'clock, she admits that no one is going to call
anyone tonight. In fact, the radio has been unusually quiet,
a sign that she is not the only one afflicted by this week of
dreary sameness—day after endless day of drizzle falling
from low beards of dark, dull cloud. The absence of sun and
lack of birdsong have combined to cloak her in joylessness,
and she feels a momentary pang of guilt. Rather than sitting
silently by, she should have reached out tonight, called
anyone, if only to ease the despondency of one or two
others.

Date: 16 Jun 23:21:56
From: Percy Turner <pturner@direct.ca>
To: gills@agt.net
Subject: About marriage and all that

Dear Gilmore,

I've never been married, and although I dream of finding someone to spend my life with, I'm not certain that a marriage would be the way I'd go. I've never wanted the ceremony or the title, only the closeness and commitment it's meant to symbolize. There are days when I think it will never happen, but life's not over yet.

Also, although it was generous of you to offer to call me on my cellphone, if you did, I wouldn't feel right. I'd always think that I should call back, and the calls would eat up a lot of what I should be saving. So, if you don't mind, I'll be a lot more comfortable if we confine our conversations to e-mail. I hope you understand.

As for the walking stick, you don't have to buy it. I'd love to give you one. In fact, I'll make one especially for you. That way, you'll owe me ;-).

Date: 28 Jun 18:45:13
From: Percy Turner <pturner@direct.ca>
To: gills@agt.net
Subject: Thinking about you, too …

You said you're getting a little high on my letters, but I think we're all just happy that the rain has stopped. Except that your letters are a welcome

Pearl Luke

diversion for me too, so part of me wants to believe you. Do you realize that we've only been writing to each other regularly for three weeks? If we had exchanged the same number of letters by snail mail—regular delivery, not monthly tower delivery—we'd have been corresponding for nearly a year already!

It scares me to think how quickly we've got to know each other, but you're right—there's magic in eliminating so many of the senses. I also like it that I get to be more articulate than I usually am; in person, I'm different, trust me.

And I really liked it when you wrote: "Accept me for all that you know of me and all that you feel, because that is all that I am." That's so true. If we'd met in person, what we knew of each other would be entirely different. That's what scares me.

ONLY an hour ago, it seemed reasonable to expect that the helicopter could haul her empty propane barrel out and bring in a new, full one. Then, cottony white clouds stood in sharp relief against a vibrant blue sky, but now the air is thick and humid, the clouds dark and ready to spill. From the helicopter dangles a lanyard that swings just beyond Percy's reach. In the past, foolishly, she has tried to jump for the lanyard when it swung too high, but she has learned to wait, her gloved hand ready.

Now, when she sees the lanyard swerve close, she reaches for the hook on the end. *Whack.* Reflexes take over, and her arm retracts. Her fingers throb as if they've just been struck with a hammer. Percy jumps back, thinking quickly. She was leaning on the iron propane pig when she reached for the lanyard, so she moves out in the open, away from the pig, and tries again. *Whack.* This time her whole arm feels the shock. She stumbles backward. When she regains her balance, she runs to the cabin.

MCJ, this is six-six-eight. Her voice breaks, comes out heavy and muffled as she chokes on spontaneous tears.

Six-six-eight, this is MCJ. Sorry about that, Percy. Looks like I picked up some static. But I just touched the cable to the ground, so we should be okay now. I want to get clear of this storm cell that's moving in.

Percy is sobbing openly and can't respond. She keys the microphone twice and runs back outside. Thunder rumbles overhead. Her hand is cautious, ready to pull back, but this time there is no shock. She slips the hook through the cable on the pig and waits until the lanyard pulls taut. With the propane tank in tow, the helicopter moves south, away from the storm.

To record where lightning strikes, if it strikes, she should already be in the tower. Instead, amazed at herself, she sits on the ground and tries unsuccessfully to choke back tears. She can't stop them, sobs bloating in her chest and then bursting forth, and it is only when the first drops of rain spatter her arms that she runs for the ladder.

Cold winds instantly replace the oppressive heat, and she climbs with difficulty, knowing that she has only seconds before the force of the storm breaks in earnest. When she is fifty feet up, a live orange-and-white current zigzags down one of four ground cables—not more than ten feet from where Percy grips the ladder. Before she can move, the sky cracks open with an enraged boom and empties itself upon her. Freezing, clothes and hair plastered to her body, she cowers indecisively. Her eardrums ache, her legs tremble and crumple inward. She clings to one rung, and even over the drum of rain on metal hears herself, pathetic, whimpering. To be in the tower for a direct hit is one thing; to be partway up the ladder is quite another. She looks up, looks down, remembers that she could be zapped at the bottom, one foot on, one foot off, and scrambles for the top. Within seconds, adrenaline moving her faster than she thought possible, she pushes through the trap door and collapses on the floor.

As soon as she recovers her strength, she stands and hastily removes her clothing, dropping everything in a soggy heap. She pulls a light flannel blanket from a shelf above one window and cocoons herself within its corners. The heavy drumming of continuous rain on the cupola drowns all other sounds, and grey sheets of water slide into the windows, driving fast-flowing rivulets through puttied seams down into puddles on the floor. Above the puddles, Percy shivers and cries, impatient with her relentless tears.

Then, as suddenly as the drop in temperature, she recalls Marlea sitting on the floor in her own hallway, big tears sliding down her face while Percy bent over her, asking, What? What? Are you all right? When Marlea couldn't answer, suddenly it was Percy who could no longer breathe. As she gasped for air, Marlea took over—her turn to console.

Here, here, breathe into the bag, breathe in, breathe in.

Percy sucked the brown paper in and out while Marlea tried to explain. A faulty plug on the clothes dryer. A jolt of 220 that had knocked her three feet and against the wall. I'm not hurt, she said, still sobbing ten minutes later, I just can't stop crying.

And now Percy understands that the jolt from the lanyard, the scare on the ladder, have given her body a shock. She gives in to the relief of tears. She lowers her chin to her chest and howls, lets her mouth hang open while she wails—for the present, and for the past as well.

She and Marlea were once so inseparable that even their dreams had been shared. At least, it seemed so when they woke to hold each other and whisper awful fears or laugh about the oddly outrageous inhabitants of their nightly visions.

Once, after they had visited Marlea's grandparents, they returned to Percy's apartment to dream that they were in a plane crash. None of the survivors had teeth, and everyone fought over the little Hershey chocolate bars Marlea's grandmother kept in a dish on the coffee table.

That's my dream, Marlea said when Percy recounted hers. I must have told you in the middle of the night.

You never told me anything, said Percy, but sometimes

when I hold you, I'm sure I know what you're thinking. Maybe now I get to share your dreams as well.

I like that, Marlea whispered, and together they fell back to sleep.

Now, just as quickly as it started, the rain slows and ceases altogether. The storm cell has moved past. Sun beats on the windows, and as the temperature rises, the windows fog, the air becomes unbearably close.

Howls no longer make sense in the quiet heat, and Percy pokes her feet and hands out of the blanket, rearranges the fabric so it hangs like a toga. She opens each of the cupola windows. Piece by piece, she wrings her sodden clothing. Finally she abandons the blanket altogether and stands naked in the sun.

July 3, 14:02. Percy can hear the blood pounding in her head as she fills the blanks on her smoke report. She has checked and double-checked the location, but she is certain she has made no mistake.

XMB four-five, this is XMA six-six-eight.

The radio operator answers immediately. *XMA six-six-eight, this is XMB four-five.*

Hi, Kim. Is the duty officer around? I have another smoke here.

It doesn't matter that she says the words calmly, matter-of-factly. Simply by sounding them, she feels the lull of a lazy Sunday afternoon collapse inward. Now it is not only the air in her cupola that crackles with tension. The whole district has been transformed by a dozen or more sets of ears perking.

Are you ready to give a smoke report?

That's affirmative. Percy reads through all of the information she has recorded on her second pink slip, then hesitates before she adds, *It's at the same location as my other fire.*

Are you sure? This is from the duty officer. *Did you have any lightning over there the other day?*

I did have some in that direction, but this is in the exact location as the last one ... northeast of twenty-three, thirty-two nine, west of the fifth.

How big is the column?

It's not even a steady column, actually, but I've been watching it for nearly half an hour, and there is definitely smoke there. More like a wisp or two every few minutes.

You're sure it's not raining over there. You're sure it's not a ghost?

To the inexperienced, mist rising from warm, damp earth looks very much like smoke. For Percy, even the question is an insult. She holds her tongue and lets the empty air time suggest what she would like to say.

Of course it's not a ghost, she says finally. *It's smoke, and it's in the same place.*

Great. Just what we need. Okay. You keep watching and tell us right away if anything changes.

That's copied. XMA six-six-eight clear.

Percy listens as the duty officer makes arrangements with the back-up officer. *We need you and Dale and a couple of the boys out there right away. And find Jake if he's around. He's not on call, but find him anyway. Can you get in with the trucks?*

It shouldn't be a problem if we take a couple of quads. The last bit is muskeg, but fairly solid, and a cutline goes straight there.

Well, get on it. Someone's head is gonna roll on this one.

The someone whose head is most likely to roll, Percy knows, is Jake, her supervisor. He was the fire-boss back in May when she first located the fire, and he was the one who got the fire under control within hours, who worked through the night in order to put it out. By noon the next day, while she was lying on her floor cradling bruised fingers, he had called in the E message that had made everyone proud and happy. E for *extinguished.* A little fire that could have gone out of control, extinguished in good time.

Except that now it isn't extinguished at all, and that is far worse than taking weeks to put it out. Someone was careless. Maybe the crew didn't dig deep enough, or maybe they didn't spot-check with their bare hands, as they should have. Percy wishes she were mistaken about the location, but she knows she is not. Through her binoculars, she sees another puff of smoke rise and disperse against the quiet blue sky.

Date: 4 Jul 07:34:29
From: Percy Turner <pturner@direct.ca>
To: gills@agt.net
Subject: re: an interesting development

Dear Gilmore,

I know. I'm so excited. I haven't had a chance to tell you this, but I've
been interested in underground fire ever since I was a teenager. The very
first one I knew about was reported on my birthday in 1966, when a guy
named Lucifer Black found a patch of ground burning on his farm near
Delburne. Turned out the fire was caused by the spontaneous combustion of charcoal in a buried pig iron furnace once used to manufacture
wrought iron. When the company went out of business, they bulldozed
and left, leaving piles of buried charcoal. Once the charcoal ignited,
flames shot out of the ground randomly until they excavated and hauled
everything away.

After that, I got interested, mostly because some religious extremists
claimed that the fire proved the existence of hell. I found more stories, and
now I have an entire scrapbook. Hell is everywhere, it turns out. Alberta,
the Northwest Territories, the U.S., Brazil, Switzerland, even in Africa.

I'm going to ask if a helicopter can pick me up sometime and fly me over
to take a look at this one. Hell on the edge of a lake. That's cool. Maybe
some kind of purgatory?

Date: 5 Jul 19:45:10
From: Percy Turner <pturner@direct.ca>
To: gills@agt.net
Subject: Religion

No. Not at all. My mother dragged me off to church a lot, but she wasn't
Catholic and I'm more sceptical than anything, so I'm no authority on
purgatory. I only thought this would be a good halfway house. Hell with a
loophole. All day in the flames but time in the water for good behaviour.
My mother had a nervous breakdown when I was a baby, and for several
months she was convinced that I was a child of the devil. That left me
more interested in the idea of hell than in the existence of God. I was also
intrigued by the idea of the devil and my mom fucking. Much more interesting than an immaculate conception, don't you think?

Date: 6 Jul 20:33:21
From: Percy Turner <pturner@direct.ca>
To: gills@agt.net
Subject: Hah!

No, my parentage is a bit complicated, but my father definitely does not
fit the role of a horny serpent. He's more of an Archie Bunker type.
Grumpy, paunchy. Always in his recliner in front of the television, TV
table beside him, beer or tea at hand. My first memories of him are
exactly the same. Maybe a different chair, but that's all. He's a good guy
all the same.

Anyway, you asked about some of the other underground fires. Most of
them are allowed to burn, unless they're really dangerous, which they can
be if roots burn away and trees topple. That's how one fire in Tennessee
was discovered—when oak and hickory trees started keeling over for no
apparent reason.

Pearl Luke

And although you heard right that some of them start spontaneously in coal veins, they're common in old mines, too. Especially in the coal tipples, where there is both coal and a pocket of oxygen. Then the bony (that's waste coal) combusts, and the fire is either allowed to burn, or all the bony is dug out and the area refilled with soil.

But not all of them are a hindrance. There's one in North Dakota called Burning Coal Vein (thanks to someone's gift for the obvious, wouldn't you say?) that has become a national tourist site. Experts think it was probably started by lightning over a hundred years ago, and it moves about ten feet a year. As the clay up above falls into the firepit, badlands are formed, like those around Drumheller, only red, so the whole area has been beautifully transformed.

Another one in Switzerland really interested me because, although warm earth is often one of the telltale signs, the temperature of the ground there was up to 385 degrees for two and a half years before they dug it up.

And in Namibia, seventy buffalo had to be shot when their hooves were burned in boiling mud!

Are you bored yet? I know you asked, but I'm afraid I'm telling you more than you wanted to know. I'll just show you my scrapbook sometime.

PERCY is euphoric. For several days she has been unable to sleep for more than a few hours at a time. She has paced up and down the length of the cabin, has walked circles around it, and is now lost deep in thought.

Already, she and Gilmore have exchanged forty-seven e-mails, some of them brief, but most long, emotional narratives about their lives and aspirations.

Gilmore is forty-two. The agency where he worked for fourteen years counselled the children of divorced parents, and he has seen what he previously supposed unthinkable. Once a father kidnapped his son and locked himself in a fifth-floor apartment with the four-year-old child. From the balcony he shouted and waved a shotgun and a bottle of whisky. A restraining order had been issued against him, preventing him from seeing both the son and the mother, and he demanded that it be rescinded. When the police closed in, he grabbed his screaming son by one ankle and dangled him from the fifth-floor balcony.

This is my son, he bellowed. He stumbled and his hold on the child slipped, but he caught himself just in time. This is my son, and nobody's gonna keep me from my son.

Firefighters spread a net below, and in time the child was safely rescued, but all Gilmore could think about for weeks after was the way people from two blocks away were drawn by the child's terrified screams, and the way his thin body went into convulsions even as the father still dangled him by the leg.

In yet another custody case, a father grabbed his teenaged daughter around the neck and forced a pistol into her mouth to hold the police at bay. He switched the gun to his other hand and held her loosely, almost lovingly, with one arm. With the other hand, he wrenched her T-shirt over her bare breasts for all the crowd to see.

She's not a child, he yelled. She's not a fucking child, and she's mine.

It was the hope of helping others that attracted Gilmore to social work. At first he thought he could make a difference, but at the end of fourteen years he had lost twenty pounds and most of his hair. He had been divorced twice, and he couldn't sleep without pills. When alcohol became more than a quick relaxant, and he was tanked more often than not, he took a disability leave and began writing the first of his two books.

Now he takes long walks along the river valley in Edmonton.

I like listening to the muffled traffic overhead, he says, and watching autumn leaves turn colour and fall sensibly free. He thinks the only thing he can change now is himself, and so he jogs in the morning and meditates in the evening.

He says he'll teach Percy how to meditate if she wants, but that meditation is organic, springing from something unique to each individual. He's found that most people yearn for release, while never realizing that release is as simple as letting go. Happiness is not about having more, he says, but about needing less.

Percy thinks about all of this as she changes the oil in her generator. Already today she has carved a lizard-like creature, deformed by the head of a human, and has flipped through several novels, unable to sustain interest in any of them. Finally, she reads one of the deleted messages from Marlea, an early one, dated May 8.

I've been thinking ...

Maybe I haven't been fair.
We can work this out. Andrew agrees ...

It is Andrew's agreement that motivates Percy to jab the delete button even before she knows to what he has agreed. The mere fact that Marlea mentions him is enough to cause her hands to shake and clench, yet she doubts her right to be angry with either of them.

Marlea is her friend. She is much more than a friend, but that is how they have always referred to each other—as friends. And friends should be supportive, not coercive. Percy believes this, and yet she cannot get beyond the short lengths of anger that band together to squeeze her chest and bind her abdomen. It is Gilmore who brings her happiness now. She'd drop him in a second if she could be with Marlea again, just the two of them forever, but she knows that is impossible.

She remembers something she saw scratched on a bathroom wall: *Happiness is only remission from pain.* Gilmore's messages bring with them that remission. When she reads his letters, her body unclenches and begins to absorb the small, glorious details of the world around her, like the joy she feels when she walks naked to the outhouse in the morning sun, confident there is not a soul anywhere to disturb her solitude. Or during spring green-up, when she first notices the soft pliability of a new poplar leaf, or sees sunstruck birds splashing in a puddle, seemingly whetting their beaks on the scent of wet earth rising. Or the happiness she felt one time that doesn't really count, when she tried antidepressants. She felt giddy for an entire week, amazed that others might spend every day laughing so easily, brushing aside minor irritations as if they didn't exist. Then, on the seventh day, something in her head gave way, maybe from the thrill of it all, and she was kept in a darkened hospital room until the throbbing behind her eyes subsided.

So what if she has never met Gilmore? It has occurred to her that he may be sending similarly intimate disclosures to others, but she has always pushed this thought to the back of her mind. He is honest and sincere, she can tell. For her own part, she has told him things she has never had the courage to share with anyone else. Not even with Marlea.

Date: 10 Jul 07:34:29
From: Percy Turner <pturner@direct.ca>
To: gills@agt.net
Subject: re: birthday greetings

Thank you for remembering! I've never received a more beautiful birthday wish. I'm only thirty this year, however, although I round up so often
I can see how you thought thirty-one. Now that I'm well into adulthood,
a year one way or the other doesn't seem all that important. Except that
I thought I would have accomplished somewhat more by now. I know
that people take pleasure from my carving, but I can't help thinking it's
not much of a career.

I wonder, sometimes, if my only purpose is to make my way through all
the years I am granted as happily and with as little conflict as possible. If
so, I'm not doing very well.

As for the underground fire, I've almost given up hope that anyone will
take me over to see it, but I guess the summer's not over yet.

I have to rush off to do my weather now, but I'm worried that I haven't
said enough about the first half of your beautiful letter. It brought tears to
my eyes, Gilmore, and if I am not responding to all that you said, at least
not in the way that you had hoped, it is only that I am stunned, and a little
nervous. I really don't know how to respond—except to say that I was
very flattered.

Pearl Luke

Date: 15 July 06:00:26
From: Percy Turner <pturner@direct.ca>
To: gills@agt.net
Subject: re: caution

Dear Gilmore,

No, please don't reserve your intensity. I like intensity.

I'm not building great walls of caution so much as I'm trying to keep at
least a weak grip on reality. Getting to know you is exciting, and if I'm
honest about all this, my thoughts are similar to yours. It's just that I'm
thinking: Are we here already, in less than six weeks? Without ever
having seen each other? I can't let this happen. I can't feel this way about
someone I don't know.

But then I get confused, because what is knowing? I know that I slept for
months with someone without ever revealing any of the thoughts and
intimacies I've already discussed at length with you.

And I take pleasure in the ways we reveal ourselves. You have to know
that, but don't forget, I haven't been with a man for nearly five years. I
don't know what I'm ready for just yet. What we have over the Internet
is exciting and invigorating and unique, but it's no guarantee we'll like
each other in person. Is it? I want to think that appearances and manner-
isms won't matter, but what if they do?

All I know is that you intrigue me and that I'm a lot happier since we
started writing to each other. Please don't stop.

Love Percy

THAT afternoon, a bird swoops into the cupola. It is thirty-three degrees Celsius, or at least it was an hour ago when Percy reported her weather, and like each day of the past two weeks, the fire hazard is extreme. Each of the eight glass window panels is open, slid completely down to encourage whatever vestigial breeze might be mustered in the thick, still air. Percy has given in to drowsiness and lies sprawled on her back in the hammock that fills an entire side of the tiny octagonal cupola. To her left is the centred wooden stand upon which the fire-finder sits; on the other side of that, a three-foot space equal to the one she fills. That's it. The cupola is an oddly shaped cell, and in it she has been spending twelve to thirteen hours a day.

The abbreviated flight of the trapped swallow wakes her as it dives madly back and forth, shrieking through a sharp, violent beak. Percy covers her head and ducks deeper down in the hammock. She is accustomed to swallows dive-bombing her in the yard, swooping past her head with only a centimetre to spare as they protect their nests, but this is madness, wings and beak everywhere, papers swept to the floor, and, unexpectedly, the sudden cool relief from a feather-breath of moving air driven by thrashing wings. Then, as suddenly as it started, the bird is out, gone, leaving nothing but oppressive stillness behind.

Percy's head throbs behind aching eyes, and little fingers of discomfort reach out to pinch awkwardly placed elbows and knees. The heat has entered her bones, and where there should be marrow, she feels instead the dull grey lead of weighted sinkers. Each minute trudges past the one before it, and a pale, listless sun drags the day forward.

Normally she likes to read in the tower, where silence is a comforting array of small, happy sounds—the wind brushing through trees or coughing up dust, birds and insects coordinating song—but even her books fail her today. The heat has been burdensome too long, and the whining of wasps and blackflies is a constant irritation.

Gilmore's last e-mail is in her back pocket and Percy pulls it out, reads it again. If only they could meet, see each other in person. She is drawn to him through his writing—clever, engaging passages designed to charm her, with each letter tentatively more intimate than the last. Tens of thousands of words, a book's worth, have passed between them already, and she feels herself submitting to these words. He flatters her, and it is his diction that seduces her as she has never been seduced, her thighs, along with her heart, opening and softening, yielding—not to him but to black ink marks on a page, signifiers, nothing more.

He says that he looks forward to sharing a glass of wine with her before a warm fire. There lie the simple signifiers, clichés of romance—the glass, the wine, the warm fire, the sharing. From these words, these things, these ideas of things, she conjures a mighty mirage—his hands lying open on the table as if wanting to prove they could never hurt her, her eyes following each vein past his wrist, up his arm, back to his heart and to what she hopes would be the beginning. With firelight in their eyes and warming their faces, they lean forward from wingback chairs across a small table, and their hands lightly brush as they speak. Her focus is on his hands again: he caresses his wine glass as if it were a breast, cups the bowl, twirls the stem between forefinger and thumb.

Do you like it? he asks, and Percy feels caught in her thoughts, glances with alarm from fingers to face.

The wine, Gilmore says, and raises a glass half-full with the indescribable colour of a good Pinot Noir.

Their faces are flushed. Hope and longing crackle between them. It is for this moment that they have waited their entire lives, this moment that is little more than a mirage spinning from the heat of words on a page.

Percy recognizes the fantasy, one of many, knows it for what it is, and yet she still feels as if she will go mad if she does not meet Gilmore soon. Tomorrow. Yesterday.

Slowly, every waking thought has become double-exposed over other slightly guilty thoughts of Gilmore. Where it used to be Marlea floating idly in the background of her mind, now it is Gilmore and he is insistent—his voice, his laughter, the memory of his words. All that jumbled up with everything else she has imagined about him. The scent of the sun on his neck, his tongue like a little pink fish in her mouth, the way his words will settle over her late at night, the way her muscles will turn to powder at his touch. If only. If only she weren't stuck here at her tower and he at his. If only the reality of their actual togetherness could live up to this seduction of words.

To take her mind off these thoughts, she reaches for the dial on her short-wave radio, hoping to pick up something, anything, that will cause an hour to pass unnoticed. What she finds are two stations, one in Spanish, and a private conversation between two people on a CB radio. The woman's voice is so heavily accented that Percy can barely discern what should be familiar words. All she hears are vowels stretched to twice their usual length.

An tharz plinty mar whar that cam fram, I tole um.

Well, that's what ya git hangin' with them all, a male voice responds. He's considerably easier for Percy to understand. *Ah tole yuh 'bout them all.*

She listens with voyeuristic interest as their exchange fades in and out, and with each word she feels ever more torpid until she tunes out altogether, dozes off again. She dreams that she is picking apples. As she drops each apple into a basket, it splits open and transforms into a knot of writhing worms, gleaming elongated maggots like those that issued from Cleopatra the day she lifted her sleek cat tail and dropped a hot, wriggling mass on Percy's chest. As large as a golf ball, the mass throbbed and began to spread and untangle, each worm rolling off Percy's body and onto her neatly made bed.

Just as a scream of terror starts in Percy's throat, just as it's ready to erupt with all the force of her lungs, static on the radio wakes her. A thin line of drool eases past her jaw and beads of sweat slide between her breasts. Her hand slicks across her cheek and, swearing softly, she sits up. The Americans are still talking, but they're fading in and out so frequently she knows she'll never determine which state they are from. They live somewhere hot, that's all she knows. Heat like this makes even the shortest vowels slow.

Through binoculars, she scans her visible area. A thin, barely perceptible fold of dark smoke hangs over a rise to the south. She has to look away, then slide her gaze back over the area slowly to be certain her eyes are not playing tricks. Her stomach does a quick flip, as if from habit, but she knows by the smoke's location and colour that this is only a quick blast from the Husky flare a few sections over. A few times a day, usually in the morning and evening but sometimes, as now, in the afternoon, she sees dark smoke from the same location. In fire tower jargon, what she sees is a permanent smoke.

Not hungry, but bored enough to eat anything, Percy roots through the drawer in the fire-finder stand until she

finds a few almonds left in a sealed bag. She washes these
down with tepid water from her thermos, already almost
empty. Having enough water is a problem on days like this,
and it is her habit to bring her thermos and an extra jug of
water up when she runs down to do the afternoon weather.
Today she forgot, and she'd rather make do with tiny sips
than check out for five minutes to rush down the ladder and
back up again.

She grabs a pack of playing cards from the drawer, and
switches from her hammock to a high swivel stool. She
pulls a wooden writing board—hidden in the fire-finder
stand like a cutting board in a kitchen countertop—out over
her lap. Here she fans cards in a game of solitaire. Every two
or three minutes, she checks for smoke. The game amuses
her for about a quarter of an hour, and then she tucks the
deck back into its box. On a shelf above her head are numer-
ous books and magazines, a small wooden puzzle—a brain
teaser she can seldom solve—an electronic chess game,
carving tools and wood, her laptop when she brings it up, as
she did today, and a handheld electronic blackjack game.

When Percy first brought the blackjack game to the
tower, a male dealer—head and torso only—was painted in
black and white above the electronic screen. With swift cold
flicks of his wrist, he dealt the cards. The severe appearance
of this image had always irked Percy, and after a few losing
games, she thoroughly resented his smug, painted stare.
First she scratched his eyes away, then his nose and square
chin. When all that remained was a thin, floating mouth
and two nondescript ears, she pored over magazines and
catalogues until she found a face she adored in just the right
size. The perky spike-haired replacement Percy glued over
the previous dealer reminds her of one of her friends, a
Japanese woman with a quick bright smile and a life so

improbable Percy would never have believed half her stories if she hadn't experienced one first-hand. The two of them went to Las Vegas once and won twelve hundred dollars playing keno, the exact amount of their combined tax bills waiting in the mail when they got home.

The replacement looks sexy in the man's narrow-waisted tuxedo and bow tie, and when Percy loses, she minds less because her new dealer merely grins saucily, her expression always the same.

At six o'clock, Percy takes a ten minute break for dinner. Before she leaves the tower, she alerts others in her area.

This is six-six-eight. I'm grabbing a bite, so I'll be down for ten.

Then she scrambles down the ladder as fast as she can. Her meal is already prepared because each night, when the hazard is high, she makes lunch and dinner for the next day and stores them in the refrigerator. All she has to do now is collect a plastic container of couscous salad, a cold Pepsi, and an apple.

After a quick dash to the outhouse, she races back up the tower and checks in to say she's on the job again. She eats dinner slowly, drawing the activity out as long as she can. She is fastidious about her apple, cutting thin slices and dabbing her mouth with a paper napkin after each bite. The evening is no more exciting than the afternoon, and not much cooler. She reads for a while and writes a few lines in her journal. Then, when she can wait no longer, Percy keys her mike.

Six-four-nine, this is six-six-eight.

She taps her pencil on the fire-finder and takes deep, long breaths to calm herself. All day she has been trying not to call Gilmore. Now it is nine o'clock and she can't hold back any longer. She rubs sweat from her forehead with her abandoned T-shirt, swipes under one bare breast, then calls again.

Six-four-nine, this is six-six-eight.

Six-six-eight, this is six-four-nine. Are you hot enough?

Now that he's answered, Percy can't think of a thing to say. She had every intention of being light and witty; she meant to reward him for answering her call, but now her hands shake and her mind is empty. *No kidding. Are you still in the tower?*

You mean we get to go down sometimes?

She detects laughter in his voice, and she laughs too, remembering to key the mike so he can hear her. *I think it's okay to sneak down after dark, over.*

Gee, I'm glad you told me. I've been up for two weeks without a break, over.

She laughs again, then pauses and takes a deep breath. *It's the same here. I haven't seen it like this for years. I've been up top from nine in the morning to ten at night every day this month.*

Me too. My fire indices are soaring. Especially the duff moisture code. My DMC is over fifty.

Fifty! Holy smokes. Things should start spontaneously combusting over there.

Don't say that too loud. That's a bit of a sore spot with the guys about now.

Well, that's probably true, but they still haven't taken me over to see that one. I'm going to start a rumour that they made up the story of an underground fire just to save their butts.

They both laugh at this and then go silent, conscious of all that they would like to say, and can't. Finally Percy keys her mike. *Did you have any build-up today?*

There is a very long pause before Gilmore says, *Sorry,*

Percy. I must have run over top of you. I asked if you had any build-up today.

I asked you the same thing.

Gilmore laughs. *Well, let's not miss an opportunity to talk about the weather! So yes, I watched several clouds build and form anvil tops, and then just when they could have crackled, the wind blew the tops off and they fell apart.*

Percy can think of nothing clever to say in reply. *Yeah. I think we must have been looking at the same ones.* She falters. *Well ... maybe we'll get some lightning tomorrow.*

I thought you had your share, over.

That was then. This is now.

I hear you. How's the wasp situation?

God, do you have them too? I've got millions of them. The hornets are down below, and the tiny ones are up here. I haven't got stung yet, but I've murdered so many I actually dreamt that a Buddhist monk was lecturing me. All these wasps were crawling on me and I was trying to prove that I really do have respect for all sentient beings. I've been having weird dreams lately.

I'm guilty of murder too, I'm afraid. There are just too many this year, over.

No kidding. And horseflies the size of baby mice. One got me in the shower and I lost a pound, more with the blood. She waits to see if Gilmore will recognize her allusion to Shakespeare. When he does, she flushes with pleasure.

From each his pound of flesh ... over.

Yes, Percy says, *but not the blood. That's not allowed.* She smiles out the window. It hardly matters what he says next. All she wants is to hear his voice, to feel it surround her. *I had a swallow in here today too. It took three swoops past my head to get back out.*

Really? I had a run-in with a black bear this morning— a big sow. I opened the door and she was only ten feet away, looking right at me. I thought she might come for the cabin when she saw me, but she was more interested in a jerry can full of gas. Over.

Percy's voice is full of concern. *Oh my god! What'd you do?*

I watched. She bit a hole in my jerry can, whacked it around a bit, and drank the gas, I think. Then she ran off into the bush. Right when I was finally going to mow my lawn too. Now I'm out of gas.

Won't it poison her?

I don't know. She seemed to like it.

Percy aims and swats a wasp. *There. I got another one. A wasp.*

Good for you. You kill the wasps, I'll watch the bears.

There is a long silence in which neither of them says anything, then Gilmore cuts back in. *I suppose we'd better not tie up the radio any more or we'll hear about it. Over.*

Reluctantly, Percy agrees and signs off, feeling more imprisoned than ever. She's certain there must be similarities between her experience and that of a prisoner—not only that she's confined in a small space day after day, as she is now, but that her choices are so narrowed she has barely any free will left to exercise. To read or look out the window. To descend the ladder and use the outhouse, or not. If she chooses the outhouse, she is obligated to call another tower.

XMA six-six-eight will be away from the radio for ten minutes. Can you cover while I'm down, please?

True, constant surveillance is only essential when the hazard is high, but it is this confinement, more than the isolation, that makes her crazy.

Yet another hornet flies into the tower. She grabs the can of Raid and follows two inches behind, spraying a steady fog of insecticide. Die, you little fucker, she says. Die.

When the hornet finally falls to the floor, she leans her forehead against a window brace and a lump forms in her throat. A spider drops and hangs at eye level. She jumps back. It is half dead from the cloud of Raid still hanging in the air, and this distresses her further. She lowers the spider outside the open window, where it can scramble away.

Date: 28 Jul 00:58:49
From: Percy Turner <pturner@direct.ca>
To: gills@agt.net
Subject: A glass of wine and a slow fire

Dear Gilmore,

I forced myself to get all my other work done before answering your note.
Now I can reward myself. And just think—only four and a half weeks until
we finally meet! I don't know how I'll stand the next month.

I can't imagine now not meeting you. When I sent my first message to
you, I thought we'd talk, that it would be interesting and fun to get to
know you. That we might become friends, possibly even good friends. I
had no idea you would fill your words with so much emotion. I don't know
how they bear the weight of all that you say.

Sometimes I think: Who is this man who can thrill me with language, for
the first time in my life? Who is this man with the wonderful voice who
can write to me so openly, who can respond so unerringly and with such
candour? With originality? With sensitivity? God, I love it, and it frightens
me so much—that I might be making you larger than you are.

THE day is warm. At nineteen degrees Celsius, perhaps it is even a bit cool for the middle of August, but Percy perspires inside a mosquito jacket, long-sleeved to save her arms from horseflies eager to nip chunks from unprotected limbs. The jacket is made from bunched mosquito netting and covers her from her knees to the top of her head, including a loose hood that fits over her hat and protects her face. She looks like the Michelin man in khaki green.

Because of the recent rain, she is spared long hours in the tower, is required only to climb at intervals for periodic checks. Instead, she scrapes at thick scabs of old paint, swears at the person who didn't do this properly last time but only painted over, spruced up, didn't care enough to prepare carefully.

Damn, she says. Damn, damn, damn. With each curse she whacks the windowsill with the wire brush and scraper, practically useless against the thick layers of baked-on paint. She's almost ready to give up and paint over, but that would be defeat, so she finds a curl of old paint separating from the wood, one more edge to slip under, and drives the scraper forward with the heel of her hand. The paint chips off, a piece the size of a quarter, and she hurls the scraper to the ground, watches it bounce on stiff bristles, then gives in to the rage that has been building for days. Her anger is not a result of anything in particular. Instead, it is the slow kindling of grievances stored over a summer that has been alternately wet and hot. In the rain she is confined to the cabin. In the heat she is forced to sit high in the tower. She has had very little time for walking and exploring, or for the sort of maintenance she is attempting now.

Percy hops down from her chair and kicks the brush farther, off into the long grass where she'll never find it.

I despise this place, she thinks, forgetting that early in the season even the scent of wet earth, or the sweet baby sweat of a peeled branch, could make her smile or hum with easy contentment. It's the only place I know, she has often said, where I have enough time. I don't rush; I don't struggle. What I don't do today, I do tomorrow, or the next day, or I never do at all. Elsewhere, hours disappear like dogs around a corner, everyone chasing, chasing, no one catching; here, time merely passes as it was intended to pass.

Yet it is true that as the summer wears on, solitude and confinement become more difficult to manage. Lately she feels that she would leave on foot, if she knew she could make her way out.

She lifts a gallon of paint out of its box, and the wide, straight brush. A whisky-jack skips to a higher branch, blackflies and mosquitoes buzz in anxious anticipation; they will hover all day for the possibility of one quick bite. The lid on the paint can isn't difficult to pry off. It lifts easily, then swivels across her wrist, leaving a streak of oil-based green.

She rubs her wrist across her hip, then wonders why she bothers. Everything always just so, always neat and tidy, ordered and neurotic. She dips the brush and pulls it along the front of her mosquito jacket, sucks in her breath, feels a rush of adrenaline, a surge of guilt, as if she's just defaced public property. She dabs the toe of each shoe, smears those against the back of each pant leg and paints the toes again.

She stares at the whisky-jack, daring it to make a peep,

then dips the brush again, this time running the bristles along the window frame—smooth, quick strokes over old paint, double-strokes over bare wood. Not defeat, but a change of heart. The edging, close to the screen, she leaves altogether. If it starts to rot, she'll change towers, go somewhere where the person painted properly—to hell with it. Small blackflies land on the paint, get stuck. She paints over them, immortalizes them in forest green.

She brushes carelessly now, inaccurately, her entire body adjusting to the furry, repetitive rhythm of the brush as it licks like an avid lapping tongue. The old paint splotches on the siding have always bothered her. When she tried one year to scrape them off, she succeeded only in adding deep new scratch marks. Today she sees the scratched splotches and understands why someone would not take time to correct their blunders, would not even see them as blunders, but only as another part of the process on a day too far into summer to care about a little extra paint on the wall.

In an hour, Percy finishes the trim on all five windows and around the door. She drags the ladder to the outhouse, and in another hour she has completed the entire job, doorframe and all. She dumps gasoline into an old coffee can and swishes the brush, bends the bristles back and forth on the bottom of the can, then brushes green gasoline on the wooden step until the brush dries.

The radio beeps. The afternoon forecast. She sits on the step to listen.

All stations, this is four-five with the PM forecast issued Friday, August sixteenth. Heavy rain continues in the east slopes and northern parks this afternoon, with the precipitation diminishing late tonight, but expected to linger in the Southeast Slopes and parks Saturday as upslope conditions persist. Some clearing in the Northwest Boreal region, but

*afternoon thundershowers and rain showers likely in most
boreal zones on Saturday. Cool and unsettled weather
continuing on Sunday.*

Percy half-listens, half-daydreams her way through the
lengthy forecast. Only at the very end does she realize that
she has missed most of what is important to her, including
the probability of lightning tomorrow and Sunday.

*Outlook for Monday: Slightly warmer with tempera-
tures in the low twenty degree range. Southeast winds ten
to fifteen kilometres per hour in most zones. Unstable and
humid with scattered afternoon rain showers and thundershowers most zones, including Southeast Slopes and parks.
Signature Nimchuk.*

Percy likes how the radio operator signs off with the fore-
caster's name. Every day, morning and afternoon, she
intones his name in the same way: her voice rises on *signature*, then after a pause she lowers it for *Nimchuk. Signature ... Nimchuk.* Very official. She unzips the hood of her
jacket, leaves the unopened bucket of white paint on the
step, and goes inside for her gloves.

The climb up the tower is long and slow. A month ago,
she would have timed herself to see how fast she could race
up the ladder. Now she climbs fifty feet and rests, continues
on to the top and drags herself through the door, all the
while calculating the number of times she's climbed this
year. Four months, thirty days a month. Four times thirty
is one hundred and twenty. Five times a day is six hundred.
Six hundred times, at least, she's climbed this ladder, and
still she's ready to drop by the time she emerges into the
cupola.

With the windows closed, the inside temperature must be
close to forty degrees. She immediately lowers one of the
eight panes of glass and hangs her head outside. Sweat

pours off her body. She detests this job. No sane person leaves her loved ones behind to sit in the middle of the forest for nearly half the year, especially when that job requires that she climb an endless ladder endless times. She'll quit next year, Percy thinks. Get a real job. Somebody else can have this one, and good riddance too.

She raises her binoculars and scans the horizon yet again, all 360 degrees, then again more slowly, zigzagging back and forth across each section of forest. Light white clouds of midday have been replaced by heavier towering cumulus, and she has a perverse desire to see them turn black, shoot dry sparks, ignite a fire or two. Maybe thrill-seekers are just people who've spent too much time alone, she thinks, people who need to balance tranquillity with terror before they go out of their minds with boredom.

For fifteen minutes she watches. Nothing. Except for that one fire and its recurrence, she's had nothing all season. *A Dry White Season.*

Now she lowers another window and stares off into the distance. She takes a deep breath and opens her mouth, letting loose a scream that is low-pitched and drawn out—a release, nothing more. She takes a second deep breath, fills her diaphragm to bursting, and tries again, this scream higher and more urgent—the sort one attempts in a dream and all too often fails to produce. She sucks more air and screams again, as loud and as long as possible until her throat scrapes and hurts, then she closes the window and hangs her head, feeling not invigorated, but somewhat silly.

The floor of the cupola is littered with dead flies, with pieces of dried grass carried up on her shoes. She lifts the trapdoor and sweeps. Dust, dirt, flies, map pins—all of it out the trap door. Finished.

She makes a move to close the other window but stops,

stares at the ground below. If she jumped carefully—used the stool to crawl up, then stood on the windowsill and pushed off—perhaps, and only perhaps, her body would sail cleanly out from the tower in a long, neat dive. If this were the case, the uneven ground would rush up to meet her finally, solidly.

But what if? What if something—a heel, a hand—got caught up in cables and crossbars, her body tumbling from one obstruction to the next, landing broken, but not incapable of further life? Sometimes Percy thinks yes, she would survive, her brains spilled, fluids oozing, the remainder of her life lived in relentless pain and humiliation. Other times, she is more optimistic and imagines a fatal landing, everything over in one sharp, decisive snap of neck or twisted spine.

Every year she reconsiders these same options, and there is nothing odd or noteworthy now in the considering; there is only the familiar uncertainty, the inability to decide, and the unwillingness to gamble on anything less than certain death. She gives her head a shake. As if even death is certain, especially suicide. She has read somewhere that victims of suicide never die, that their souls live forever, trapped, as in life, in an otherworld of their own making.

With a last wistful look, she closes the window and starts back down the ladder. Bang. Rattle. The angle iron plays its usual tune. Ninety-eight, ninety-nine, one hundred. Her shiny green toe touches the ground.

SHORTLY before nine o'clock that evening, the sound of a helicopter rouses Percy from an early retreat inside her mosquito net. At first she ignores the muffled thuds, certain that the chopper will fly over. As it gets nearer, she knows she is wrong. This one is landing. She peers out the kitchen window, feeling like a small animal in a threatened nest. The radio remains quiet, so whoever it is, he or she is not on forestry business.

Gilmore! she thinks. Of course. Ever since he mentioned that he'd do anything to visit, Percy has been secretly hoping he would find a way. But now, of all days! She is unwashed, painted, puffy with self-pity. She'd be ashamed to greet a stranger looking like this; to meet Gilmore for the first time is unthinkable. Her spirits plunge, then soar again, her heart beating so fast she's afraid she'll faint before she has a chance to tidy up. Her hands are everywhere—collecting, cleaning, pulling at her hair.

She takes a peek out the window and sees a small black-and-white helicopter landing in her clearing. Two people are seated up front, but the sun glints off the glass bubble, distorting her view. Although she wishes she could see what he looks like, she has no time to waste watching. His appearance means little to her now anyway. He could look like a goat or a god; she would be equally excited to see him, or so she hopes.

She pours water into the washbasin and scoops handfuls onto her face, drying with the inside of her shirt as she dashes into the bedroom for her good jeans and a clean blouse. As she pulls them from hangers, she sees her reflection in the mirror and green streaks running through her hair. She brushes madly, jerks hard on the tangles, but the green straggles remain. Finally, knowing she must either rip clumps out by the roots or ignore the paint entirely, she gives up and secures her hair with a bright elastic at the nape of her neck.

Her heart still beats double-time, and she has broken into a light sweat. Why didn't he e-mail to let her know he was coming? She could have been ready. But it doesn't matter. He has come; somehow he has come.

She struggles with her jeans. To save time, she tried to slip her foot through the leg with the shoe still on. Now she is afraid she will be caught like this, undressed, dancing a wild and unstable hop as she tries to free her foot. With effort, she pulls the shoe off while it is still inside her pant leg. She pulls her own leg back and feeds her arm down into the jeans to retrieve the shoe.

The helicopter is not shutting down, a sign that it will take off again soon. They will have no time to adjust to the sight of each other. No small talk with someone else to act as a buffer between them. Percy can barely breathe. She pulls the curtain aside to take another look. As she does, she hears a knock, barely audible over the engine of the chopper.

She kicks off the other shoe and pulls her jeans over her hips. I'm coming, she yells. Thank God she locked the door. Her fingers are frantic, but finally she zips her jeans in place. She feels as if she could throw up any second.

The doorknob jiggles. A rap on the window by the door. Is anyone there?

At the sound of this unfamiliar voice, Percy sucks in her breath and stops halfway across the room. Her disappointment is swift, but even as she chokes back the hurt, she is flooded with relief. She approaches the door cautiously.

Beads of sweat stand out on her forehead, and she swipes them away before turning the knob.

I didn't think you were here, the man says.

Percy gives a short laugh, recognizing him as one of the pilots from another district. Where would I go?

The man shrugs and holds a few letters out to her. Guess you've got a point there.

Percy takes the bundle of mail. Can you come in? she asks, although she already knows the answer. The passenger she saw from the window is still in the chopper.

Can't. No. We're on our way to Yellowknife. But the gal in the office figured you might need those. You've got one there that looks important.

Percy shuffles the envelopes. Scrawled across one, in Marlea's hand, is the word URGENT in double-bold letters. On the back, the letters are underlined: OPEN IMMEDI-ATELY. DEATH IN FAMILY.

Percy's heart nearly stops. She steps back and reaches for the wall.

You okay? You want me to wait?

No, Percy says. Then, Yes. Sure. Please. She leans against the wall and opens the letter with shaking hands.

She unfolds two typed pages, then reads quickly: *Sorry, Percy. I know I've probably scared you, but there is no death. I just didn't want you throwing this out before you read it. My uncle was in a serious accident though, so don't be too hard on me.*

Percy feels blood rushing back into her face. Of all the manipulative tricks. This pilot, and the people in the office—all of them worried that she get the letter right away. She sets her front teeth together and continues staring at the page while she decides what to do next.

When she looks up from the letter, she rubs the space between her eyes.

Bad news?

Yes. Percy glances at the pilot, then away. A friend, she says. My friend's father died. But we knew it was coming. He was in a lot of pain.

Cancer?

Percy nods. There's nothing I can do from here, but I appreciate your bringing this by. She waves the letter and tries to smile. Thanks. I'm fine now.

You're sure then?

Percy nods again and raises her hand in farewell. She waits until he's off the step before she closes the door, then she marches to the desk and grabs her telephone. She stabs each of the eleven numbers, then waits for the long distance connection.

Marlea's answering machine picks up on the fourth ring. *Hi, this is Marlea, and no one is available to take your call. If you want to leave a message for me, please do so after the tone. If you want to leave a message for Andrew, press one now.*

Percy presses the cancel button with her thumb. That's the trouble with cell phones. There is no receiver to slam when you need one.

She twists her wristwatch until she can see the face. It is nine-fifteen. Marlea is a chef. She would have left for work at five. She won't be home until one or two in the morning. Andrew is also a chef. He works at the Elks club, and he is just as likely to be on the golf course as in the kitchen.

Percy fingers the letter suspiciously. Her brain hums with little inconsistencies. As often happens with Marlea, Percy wants to feel angry but is not certain she has the right. She slumps at the table and smooths the pages flat to read the rest of the letter.

I know you'll remember Uncle Blair, Dad's brother in Saskatchewan. He crashed his plane early this spring, just after you left for the tower. I've been trying to let you know, but you didn't respond to my letters or my e-mail, and every time I phone, I get the same automated message, so I'm guessing that you haven't read anything I've sent.

Anyway, the short version is that I took some time off work and we—Mom, Dad, and I—have spent most of the summer out in Saskatchewan trying to help Uncle Blair. For a while we didn't know if he'd make it, and it's been really hard, especially for Dad. For me too. I think this was the first time I really understood that my parents won't be around forever. Dad always seems so young, but he looked about ninety sitting by Uncle Blair's hospital bed.

What happened was that he took off from the grass runway on his farm and then suddenly crashed in the neighbour's fallow. The neighbours heard his engine sputter and stall, and the guy and his son raced out to the field. They were able to drag Uncle Blair away from the plane, but then the whole thing went up in flames. Dad still gets choked up whenever he talks about it. Thinking about the close call, I guess.

I thought I knew my uncle fairly well, but now I don't think I know anything about him. Once we were there, we found out he was flying to San Francisco for the weekend. By himself. Doesn't that make you stop and think about why he never married? It made me think, and sure enough, he visits Montreal every once in a while too. I asked Mom if he was gay and all she said was: Could be. We've never thought it was our place to ask him. As if he wouldn't be as eager to talk about his life as anyone else, but I didn't say anything to her. I didn't feel it was my place to ask him either, so who am I to criticize? And now I can't stop thinking about how I'll feel when Mom and Dad are gone. I love them both so much.

And you know what Mom said when we were out in Saskatchewan? She said, It must be hard on you when Percy goes away every summer. Don't you just feel like one of your legs is missing? So then I broke down and told her how I hadn't been able to talk to you all summer, and how I feel like I'm going to go crazy if we don't talk soon, and she just held me for a long time the way she used to when I was a kid.

Maybe it's time, she said, to figure out what you're going to do about that girl.

I wasn't sure what she meant exactly, and I was going to ask, but then the moment passed. A bit later, I was talking about you again, and she said something that almost knocked me over. She said, very quietly: You know I like Andrew, he's always good to us, but you don't love him the way you love Percy. I hope that's as obvious to you as it is to us.

Then Dad came in and she said, I just hope you're being honest with yourself, honey, that's all. Then they started talking and we never did come back to that subject. Can you believe it? I always thought they'd disown me if they thought I was queer. Although they've always been great about everything. Maybe I just didn't want to test them.

So now I don't know anything any more. All I do is go to work and sleep. Go to work and sleep. I'm trying to decide if Mom's right about Andrew, and if you're right about me using you—and I feel so bad. I do love you, Percy. I know I love Andrew too, in a different, less passionate way, but maybe Mom's right—if I have to lose anyone, I don't want it to be you.

Percy stops reading. Outside, she can still hear the heli-copter flying away. Over the years, she has come to associ-ate this receding whine with a mixture of sadness and relief. Now there is no relief, just a layer of shame. She should have read Marlea's letters. She should never have thrown them out.

AT first Percy wants to pick up her telephone and call until she reaches Marlea, wants to comfort her and apologize and breathe her grateful love into Marlea's familiar ear. But she won't allow herself. Things are different now. Much different. She will be meeting Gilmore in less than two weeks, and already—however much they have questioned this rush to claim each other—they feel like soulmates. She knows this sounds like an Internet cliché, like some chat room love affair destined to fizzle on first sight, but the knowing fails to negate the bond they have already established. They've mentioned love. They've made plans. A month ago she could still have turned away from all that. Today, she's not so sure.

Besides, Percy has begun to realize that she has every right to be angry with Marlea. Gilmore has helped her to understand that Marlea takes the track of least resistance, always. Even now, it is only her mother's nudging that has allowed Marlea to say that she would choose Percy over Andrew. At least, this is what Percy believes Marlea has said. Maybe not as clearly as she would have liked, but close enough that she felt her hopes jump and bump when she read Marlea's words. Jump, as her hopes began to ascend, then bump as they landed again. For what kind of a commitment is Marlea offering really? *If I have to lose anyone, I don't want it to be you.*

All her life, Percy has been in love with Marlea. After that first time by the river, she thought they would continue to be physically intimate, spending hours twined together, each discovering herself in the other, and discovering the differences too. She felt as if they had just opened the window on a secret garden and found ivy and birds. Sunflowers and an ancient urn. But Marlea would have none of that.

It's narcissistic, she said. It's not natural. It's as if we're so in love with ourselves we can't even bear to be with the opposite sex.

But that's ridiculous, Percy said. I love you. I've been with boys, and I could be with them now, but I'd rather be with you. You're my best friend, *and* I go all queasy just sitting next to you. Besides, you don't look anything like me.

It's not that we *look* the same. It's that we *are* the same. Breasts, hips, skin, vagina. You know. All of it. It's not natural. I'm not a lezzie.

There was that word again. Said in the same tone as when Marlea first suggested that Mrs. Miller might be a lesbian.

They were sitting on a sand spit beside the river. Percy toyed with a stone Marlea had found for her and pressed into her hand earlier in the day—a smooth, flat rock half the size of Percy's palm, and heart-shaped.

Percy waited until she knew Marlea had seen how lovingly she caressed her gift, until she saw from the slight bend of Marlea's lips that she was pleased at how much Percy liked the stone. Then she stood and walked to the water's edge.

Have it your way, she said over her shoulder. She turned, pausing until she was certain that Marlea watched her, and she skipped the rock across the water. Four, five, six times it skipped before plopping softly into the river, sinking and disappearing forever. I still think it's a stupid reason, she said.

She had always deferred to Marlea, but finally to have everything she longed for, only to have it taken away again, was too much. She hoped Marlea's heart would turn as grey as the vanished stone, as grey as her own.

Then there was the day of Uncle George's funeral. Percy was twenty-three, freshly graduated from Alberta College of Art. Marlea still attended the Southern Alberta Institute of Technology, right next door to the art college. She loved to cook, and she excelled at it, had won awards.

They had moved to Calgary together, and when they first arrived, they lived in a condo overlooking the river. The place was cheap in those days, and Percy chose it because the manager mentioned that a previous owner had sculpted there before she became well known and moved to a larger studio. Secretly, Percy hoped that talent and renown would linger in dust and sand particles; she hoped to be spared, in her own carving, the fate of unoriginal thought or boring design.

The apartment had two bedrooms, and if Percy bought groceries, Marlea cooked. When she cleaned the bathroom, Marlea vacuumed. From Percy's perspective, the arrangement worked perfectly, but Marlea didn't agree.

We spend too much time together, she said. We need to meet other people and do more on our own.

But why? Percy argued. I'm happy the way we are.

It's not right, Marlea said, and not long after that she moved to a neighbouring building.

Still, she was the first to hear the message from Percy's mother. She let herself in with her old key, and while she waited for Percy, the phone rang. She listened as the answering machine recorded the news.

This is Mom. I need to tell you about Uncle George. He's gone, so phone me when you get home. This is Mom. Bye.

He's gone, her mother had said, her voice breaking on that word, and Percy knew right away that this time Uncle

George had died. Walking to get his mail, of all things. A heart attack. His first, and his last. Still, the news came as a surprise. She thought that her parents' contact with him had ended all those years ago when he left Oldrock. Now all of the unanswered questions of her adolescence rose up like swift, morbid shadows, and with them came the phrase *child of the devil*, playing over and over like unbidden song lyrics in a relentless loop.

There was a message from a lawyer too, and Percy and Bobby arrived at the reading of the will together while Marlea waited in the reception area, sitting straight and thin on a plush-bottomed chair. Also present in the lawyer's office was Mrs. Dumphrey, introduced to them as the sister of the deceased, and her husband, Mr. Dumphrey. No first names were offered, but Mrs. Dumphrey had the same unruly red hair and amber-flecked eyes as Percy, at whom she looked with unconcealed distaste.

The lawyer raised his eyebrows when he learned that Bobby and Percy had never met the Dumphreys, but what did he care? Percy thought. As clients, she, Bobby, and the Dumphreys had to be less than inconsequential.

Looks as if there's about thirty thousand in savings and investments that will be divided between you two, he said, directing his comment to Percy and Bobby. The will also states clearly that the net proceeds of the estate, consisting primarily of two older vehicles and a small home, will be divided equally between the three of you. Anyone could see that the lawyer wanted to appear concerned, and this time his look included Mrs. Dumphrey. Are there any questions? Do any of you need anything clarified? Anything at all?

I have a question, Percy ventured. Does it say anything in the will about his relationship to us? She blushed pink, but she met the attorney's brown-eyed gaze.

He was the first to avert his eyes. He spent a moment shuffling through the will and then raised his eyebrows. I assumed you would know that relationship. He looked from Percy to Bobby. All I have here are your names.

That's okay, Percy said. She lowered her head and bit the side of her lip. I just wondered if it said anything else.

It says you get the bulk of his money, Mrs. Dumphrey said. I'm sure you can figure out why.

Percy just stared. The woman—her aunt, she supposed—was like a chihuahua barking from a safe distance. She chose not to respond. Uncle George had taught her that. Always remember, he said, that often the most memorable thing you can say is nothing at all. A lot of people don't know how to respond to nothing.

Maybe he had a lifetime of practising with his sister, and with a sudden blurring of her eyes, Percy realized that she would never know. Earlier, she had gone to the funeral home alone, and it had been a shock to see Uncle George laid out in a casket with his hands folded and still. He was only fifty-five when he died, but in death he looked old, his powdered flesh no more natural-looking than flesh-coloured Crayola.

She remembered that he taught her to carve, gave her a little pearl-handled jackknife she still kept in a drawer. She had forgotten how he sat with her on the step, and how those same hands, warm and gentle, had guided hers while he showed her how to make a whistle from a chunk of green willow. Later, he divided a cedar shake into strips a half-inch square by about a foot long. He taught her to use a series of v-cuts to slice into the soft wood and demonstrated how, if she repeated the cuts at different angles, they would eventually form an intricate pattern.

Before he went away, she used to slide her smaller hand

into Uncle George's big one and sit quietly, listening to his jokes until her mother shooed her away, but at the funeral home, when she reached out to stroke his fingers for the last time, they were as cold and unresponsive as the skin of an uncooked fowl. For hours after, his chill clung to her, and she was certain she had stolen some part of him he needed—as if, having died, he could spare nothing more. She washed her hands and dried them, then ate potato chips but couldn't lick salt from her fingers because she still felt him there.

His sister could have been a link to all that was warm and rooted in him, to the aspects of himself that would continue to live and grow in others, but when the lawyer finished, the couple rose without a word. Mr. Dumphrey followed behind his wife as they silently made their way toward the office door. He shook the lawyer's hand and merely nodded at Percy and Bobby.

You have yourselves a good day, Bobby said. He spoke in an uncharacteristically loud voice, and with a wide loose gesture he waved his hand above his head. See you at Christmas and Easter, folks.

Percy elbowed him in the ribs. Have some respect.

Why? He looked at his sister and shook his head. Exactly what is there about those people that makes you want to be nice?

LATER that evening, Marlea ran Percy a warm bath, massaged oil into her muscles, and stayed, holding Percy in her arms. Percy had never been happier.

Do you feel better or worse? Marlea asked. Knowing about your uncle?

Percy took a minute to distinguish between the levels of satisfaction that fed her overall sense of well-being. I was a bit sad this afternoon, but my parents are still my parents, and it makes me happy to think that I came from Uncle George's gene pool. His sister wasn't showing her best side, but he was never like that. Every memory I have of him is a good one. And I always wondered where Bobby got his sense of humour. Now I know. But I still wish my parents had told us. Maybe things could have been different.

Maybe. Marlea sounded doubtful. Are you going to ask them why they didn't?

Percy shook her head. No. I think your mom was probably right when she told me that some answers are more trouble than they're worth.

Good thinking, Marlea said. She rolled over and pulled Percy's mouth to hers. Then, vehemently, I do love you, you know.

I know, and I'm glad you stayed. It means a lot to me.

For the rest of the night, Percy hardly slept, just lay with her cheek pressed against Marlea, memorizing her softness, feeling her flesh as near to her as her own whirling thoughts. No one knew her as well as Marlea, and just being next to her, Percy felt as if the whole of the earth had risen inside her.

In the morning, despite her lack of sleep, she felt buoyant

with energy. She dressed carefully in a navy blue pantsuit and woke Marlea.

Marlea ran home to get ready, but she returned so that the two of them could share a taxi to the funeral.

I'm going to buy my condo, Percy said. With the inheritance, my mortgage will be less than rent. Her grip on Marlea's hand tightened. They told me it was for sale if I ever wanted to buy, and now I do. You can live there again too, if you want.

Marlea squeezed back and smiled.

When the taxi pulled into the parking lot, there were unfamiliar faces everywhere.

Marlea craned her neck. There's Andrew, she said.

Before the car came to a complete stop, she had her door open. Andrew! Marlea waved her purse in the air and repeated his name until Andrew saw her and started toward them.

Percy's face went pale. What's he doing here?

You remember Andrew? He's in my cooking class.

They had encountered him in the park a few weeks before, and Marlea had gone all silly and flirtatious.

I remember who he is, Percy said. I just don't understand why he's here.

Marlea narrowed her eyes. I asked him. She faltered. I asked him when we first found out. I just assumed you'd want to be with your family, that I'd need someone to sit with. Your parents don't exactly make me feel welcome.

You *are* family, Percy said, but Andrew had already made his way over to them.

Hi. He held Marlea's gaze that extra moment, the way new lovers often do, and then he turned, too late, to Percy. I'm so sorry, he said. Marlea told me about your father.

Percy would not return his smile, would not even correct

him. Instead, she turned blank eyes to Marlea and slid back in the cab. I'll see you inside, she said. She waited until they started toward the funeral home, then she spoke to the cab driver. My uncle's already dead. I don't think he'll mind if you take me back downtown.

PERCY is certain she would have given up these summers at the tower if Marlea had truly wanted her. She's tired of the long climb and the isolation. More than anything, she is tired of feeling lonely. Not in the usual way, as now, when the season is nearly over and she's desperate for human contact, but in general. She is surprised at how the smallest thing—a ladybug on the back of her hand, or the hammering of a woodpecker deep in the woods—can cause her to recall circumstances far in the past.

Unless she consciously focuses, her mind makes a jumble of time. Memories get mixed with present events as well as with her hopes for the future, and with so many snippets of thought coming and going at a disconcerting rate, she's not always certain where she resides in time, or how distorted the facts have become. For distorted they are. Of that she is certain.

She has caught herself reconstructing events, adding clever retorts she wasn't quick enough to make, paraphrasing to bring herself off as more articulate than she was. She's also aware of how often she edits anything that resists her notion of self—whatever notion of self she finds appealing at the moment, that is. More than once she has deleted a nasty jab that made her seem unkind, a thoughtless or insincere comment at odds with the kind of person she wishes she were.

She used to think loneliness was good for her, that it strengthened her character, but she sees now that being lonely only makes her feel sad and angry. When she is alone, she finds it easier to blame others than to discover the root problems in her own behaviour, and isolation has only served to postpone self-awareness and change, not to advance them, as she once supposed.

She spends all these months at the tower, thinking about everything that has ever happened or will ever happen, and just when she thinks she has everything worked out, she goes back to Calgary, only to discover that the reason everything worked so well in her imagination was because solitude left no room for anyone to challenge her. All that growth, nothing but an illusion.

IN the early hours of the morning, Percy dreams that she is at the beach with Marlea. The ocean air is thick, filled with Mexican images. There are scorpions and fantailed fish swimming in terra cotta pots, and geckos flicking across the veranda. Flit and freeze. Tongues in and out. Heat so dense that only geckos can stop and start so quickly. Percy is wearing no clothes and can feel warm sand along her back as her nipples point into the sun. Strangers spread her arms and legs, happy to caress her until she brushes them aside. She captures sand crabs, hunched like old people, and tickles their legs into action with whistles of breath that send them scurrying upward from her navel.

They'll pinch, Marlea says.

Instead, they scoot up bare fleshy hills and rises until, atop a shoulder or skittering too quickly down a slope, they fall to familiar ground and scuttle away like large armoured spiders.

Marlea strokes Percy's arms too, with wide brown fingers nothing like the ones Percy knows so well, their smooth tips sending shivers into her hairline all the same.

I want you permanently near, Marlea whispers, while a backdrop of water shimmers and reflects an everchanging range of translucent pastels throughout the day. Even when darkness drops around them, they are safe and content listening to the sound of crickets and gecko chuckles, and to the steady heave of the ocean that never ends. Under a light bulb in the distance, the faint sound of glass clinking invites them, and any notion of loneliness washes out with the sand.

Percy licks salt from Marlea's lips, then licks her own lips, is still licking them when she opens her eyes to the early morning. She feels as happy and as aroused as she has ever been. She disentangles herself from her covers and leaves bed reluctantly.

She logs on to the Internet as usual. There is a message from Gilmore.

Date: 17 Aug 06:50:42
From: Gilmore A. Graham <gills@agt.net>
To: pturner@direct.ca
Subject: Happy Saturday

I'm up early and wanted to wish you a good morning. And to say that wherever we may find ourselves physically, my thoughts will forever be coupled with yours. Only two more weeks!

Love, Gilmore

Percy frowns at the walls around her. He is intruding somewhere between the beautiful beach she just left and the cheap wallboard that surrounds her, and the contentment that dominated her dream is slipping away. She wants to demand sleep again, to re-enter that world where everything was exactly as she wished. But she is running late. The dream is over. Likewise, any message back to Gilmore will have to wait until later. She saves his message, then logs off and grabs her gloves.

Later in the morning, she rereads the e-mail and cringes. Yesterday, his message would have moved her, and she would have written back immediately. Today, his words seem too strong, too intense for the time they have corresponded, yet weak, weak, weak, compared to the emotions in her dream. Marlea sometimes accuses Percy of being fickle. Obviously she is.

She has sent dozens of messages like Gilmore's herself, all of them equally intimate, each one filled with proclamations that suddenly seem so overwrought as to be nothing less than ludicrous. With all her concerns about what was real and what was not, why did it never occur to her that she might instantly, sensibly, regret everything she foolishly put in writing?

She gives her head an impatient shake, trying to rid herself of the sensation that Marlea is in the room with her. Marlea cannot be exorcised so easily, and neither, Percy sees, can lasting love be conjured out of a keyboard.

She's heard about people who have gone crazy at the tower, wandering off into the bush, hallucinating, hanging themselves. Maybe this is how craziness begins, when reality is forfeited to dreams and when the boundaries between the two are no longer certain. Or is insanity easier to recognize?

Would she imagine that the spiders in the cupola were plotting against her, all of them watching her with beady black eyes, waiting until they could attack at once, swarming her with hundreds of horrid bloated bodies atop scuttling furry legs? Would she gouge scabs off old mosquito bites and save them in an envelope? Maybe she'd record the number of dandelions on her lawn, numbering them in the thousands, or pull all the hairs from her arms, one at a time, counting them up—she loves me, she loves me not. Perhaps she'd sit perfectly still and imagine the symptoms of a deranged mind, as she is doing this minute.

Certainly she would feel fragile, as she feels now. Again, she gives her head a shake. This can't continue. Perhaps a walk will help.

XMA six-six-eight is going for a walk. I'll be away from

the radio for an hour or so. Percy's voice sounds even on the radio, but she holds it steady through sheer will.

Her head aches from thinking about Gilmore and trying not to think about Marlea, so she forces herself to focus on the colours and scents in the lane, now lined with hundreds of wild roses, bluebells, and yarrow. She is in a premenstrual slump. She must be. No energy. Critical. Too emotional. Aroused by nothing more than the seam of her jeans while she walks.

Why is it that, with all of the medical breakthroughs, no one has yet discovered a way for women to empty themselves of their menstrual flow in one simple evacuation? Even she can imagine a tiny vaginal or intrauterine vacuum that would suck her clean in seconds. Enemas were easy enough, as were suction hoses for dentists. What can possibly be so complicated about menstruation that she is still obliged to bloat and leak every twenty-eight days? Why won't someone attend to this colossal oversight?

Wanting what she can't have is a habit she has perfected over the years, and one she wishes to dislodge. She'd like to love Marlea the way cats love their owners, going to her uncritically and without reserve to soak up affection, eliciting warm responsiveness from Marlea, then leaving without concern when the moment is over. How wonderful to simply remove oneself, nonchalant and catlike, the way friends do.

Instead, however much Percy has removed herself physically, her mind continues to hang on, not at all friendlike. Yet to write or call Marlea and ask outright if anything has changed would also mean to let go, to make herself vulnerable one more time. She can't do that. She would be foolish to do that.

Some of Percy's friends think that Marlea is selfish and

manipulative. And homophobic, of course. But Gilmore has discussed this with Percy. These observations are only true from a certain perspective, and whether or not Percy agrees, Marlea owes her nothing. Nor is Percy's happiness dependent on the love of another. Happiness is possible, Gilmore says, with neither love nor approval, with neither talent nor purpose. Happiness is possible alone, and it requires nothing more than a receptive mind.

He makes mental health sound so easy. He makes contentment sound so easy, and yet for her it is not.

After an hour of walking, Percy is thinking no more clearly than she was when she began. Certainly she is no happier. Yesterday she knew what she wanted—Marlea was out, Gilmore was in. Now that certainty is gone, ploughed under by something as nebulous and disconcerting as a cheerful dream.

FACED with steady rain in the afternoon, Percy gives in to her lethargy, burrowing deep into the comforting warmth of her bed, where she wraps the sheet around her head like a baby's caul and hopes for nothing more fortunate than sleep. When she wakes the next morning, and each day after, to the persistent drumming overhead, she experiences her only pleasure—the knowledge that she will not have to climb the tower for another day.

Immediately after reporting her weather each morning, she retreats under the covers again, her thoughts stuck in some confused tumble of memories, the same thoughts round and round, none of them singular and clear. She wishes she could set each memory up on display, walk around it, kick it, check it for signs of wear, for flaws she hadn't noticed until now, then relive it and let it go, but the effort needed to concentrate only puts her back to sleep so she can wake later, grateful that a few more hours have passed.

For an entire week, Percy does little except record and report the weather. Rather than walk to the outhouse, she pees in a bucket and throws the contents into the rain once a day. She stops showering and only forces herself to eat a bowl of cereal and milk when the effort of getting out of bed causes her to clutch at the wall, pale and clammy with dizziness. The cabin takes on a musky animal smell with the windows closed; she doesn't notice and would not care if she did.

Let me introduce my selves, she thinks, wondering how Gilmore might respond to such an apathetic and weak version of herself, an imitation of the person who sat at the computer typing sincere, effusive replies to his electronic messages. Or perhaps that person is an imitation of this one. She no longer knows.

She drifts in and out of sleep, and when she is awake, her mind wanders so that she can't recall what she was thinking from one moment to the next. She often finds herself fingering the silver and gold band on her little finger. She and Marlea each have one, and Percy has worn hers for so long that the ring rotates in a shallow groove worn into her flesh. For years she has protected the band as a meaningful symbol. Now she thinks she might just as well have left it in the campground outhouse where she once threw it.

She remembers being so angry she wanted to drive back to the city without Marlea, wanted to leave her to find her own way home with the borrowed tent and the dull axe that neither of them could swing with any effectiveness.

Be with me, Percy had said, nestled against Marlea in the privacy of that heavy, mouldy tent. Like this, forever.

In a canvas tent? Marlea joked, slapping at a mosquito. In a modified yurt with the mosquitoes bloating themselves on our blood?

Percy lifted her face, only half-amused and unwilling to let the matter drop.

I can't, Marlea said. I don't know why, I just can't. She rolled the blankets around her, cutting herself off from Percy. We spent too much time together as kids, that's all. Now it's hard to stop—

And you want to stop? Percy was not asking facetiously. She wanted to know.

No. I don't think so ... I don't know.

And so Percy found herself stomping along the gravel loop that connected each camping site to the next. There were no dead ends anywhere, only neat one-way traffic circles keeping every camper in her numbered place. She responded with curt nods to the silent and friendly head-tipping of middle-aged strangers passing her on the road. Finally, wanting only to be alone, she darted into the nearest outhouse.

There, oblivious to the odour, to the spiderwebs and flies, unaware that the sweet mossy bank of the river was only a few feet away through the trees, Percy sat on the toilet seat, twisting her ring in its groove of flesh while hot tears dribbled down her cheeks. Marlea gave her the ring on a trip to Mexico. Ten dollars for two sleek gold and silver bands bought in a shop along a well-swept cobblestone street. Unintentionally they had acted in unison as they each slid a ring on a baby finger, and although the band was never meant to signify a pledge of any sort, the joint sliding on communicated a strong and unspoken sense of commitment. Although Marlea was already dating Andrew, Percy read her acknowledgement of the ring's significance in her shy laughter, in the way she squeezed Percy's hand after, and in the way neither of them spoke of the action, as if speaking might risk something already too tenuous.

Remembering all this, Percy sat in the outhouse, hurt swelling into mute rage because she knew how foolish she was to want something from Marlea that Marlea could not give. If Percy was *enough*, if she was interesting enough, sexy enough, lovable enough, wouldn't they be together already, as a couple, rather than as secret and occasional lovers?

Percy twisted the band from her finger, raised the toilet seat, and flung the ring into the hole.

You can go to hell, Marlea, and fuck Andrew too.

For a moment, she stood staring after the ring. She had

the idea that she should have at least made a wish, and she felt a strong desire to laugh, although she had never felt less amused. Then she broke out in a sweat that had nothing to do with the humid late-afternoon heat. Her ring lay at the bottom of the hole, a tiny glint in a pit of stinking filth.

Marlea was seated outside on a folding chair, reading a book, when Percy returned. Finished with your little tantrum, are you? she asked, not bothering to lift her head.

Percy said nothing.

Marlea flipped a page of her book and looked up. She knocked her chair aside in her rush to get to Percy. What is it? What happened to you?

Tearfully Percy held her unadorned right hand out in front of her body for Marlea to see. I threw my ring in the toilet.

A flicker of surprise, then impatience, crossed Marlea's face. What? Why—

Because I'm an idiot. Percy covered her face with her hands. I didn't mean to throw it in. I mean, I did, but as soon as I did I wished I hadn't. She let her hands drop. Will you help me get it back? Please?

From down the outhouse? Marlea shook her head. They weren't expensive. I'll buy another one.

You can't buy another one. Not from the same place. Percy's eyes pleaded. It wouldn't be the same. They were special.

God, Percy. We can't get it out.

We can. Maybe. If no one's covered it up. If no one's used the toilet—

Marlea tilted her head back and laughed. She stepped forward and pulled Percy into her arms. What do you want me to do, hold you by the ankles and lower you down the hole?

Percy could feel Marlea's body shaking with laughter. She pushed her away and twisted free. This is serious, she snapped. She went to the cardboard box resting on the far side of the picnic table and rooted through their camping supplies. There's got to be something we can use—

C'mere, Marlea said, arms out, face as serious as Percy's. Okay. I'll help.

Fifteen minutes later they had devised an instrument of rescue from a plastic mug, a long branch, a clothes hanger, and duct tape. Marlea lowered the contraption down the hole while Percy shone a flashlight beam onto the ring, still visible atop a pile of soggy, stained toilet paper.

I've almost got it, Marlea said. She poked around in the pile of tissue and excrement until the lip of the cup slid under the edge of the ring. I'm going to have to bring a lot of other crap up with it, but I think I can get it.

A fly settled on Percy's forehead, but she didn't even attempt to swat it away. Her whole attention remained focused on holding the light steady, on not doing anything that might send the ring sliding out of sight forever.

I've got it!

Percy bit down on her lip to stop her tears. She felt as if she, and not merely the ring, had just been rescued. She held the flashlight steady and choked out the first words that came to mind. We can throw the cup back.

Well, no kidding! Unless you thought we might use it again?

Involuntarily, Percy laughed. Everything would be all right now. It was enough that Marlea was with her—more than enough. She grinned and kicked the door open, holding it wide as Marlea backed out into the sunlight, balancing the cup.

Another camper walked by on the road and shot them an odd look. Marlea and Percy nodded politely, then looked at each other and broke into giggles. It was a conspiratorial moment, almost as significant as the one they shared when Marlea first purchased their rings. For all the years Percy had loved Marlea, she had never loved her more fervently than at that moment.

Marlea tipped the cup, dumping the contents to the ground, and Percy squatted, snatching the precious band from between clumps of soaked toilet tissue. She slid the ring back on her finger and reached for Marlea.

Oh no, you don't! Marlea backed off and held the pole between them. Don't even think about touching me. Not until you've scrubbed.

PERCY'S smile is sad as she recalls the expression on Marlea's face, until she realizes that she has just followed an entire memory through to its end. Although she is still propped up in bed, she is no longer sleeping all day, every day. Her thoughts are more orderly, and confusion has been replaced with a feeling of resigned emptiness. She has spent her whole adult life wanting Marlea to love her completely, to commit to her, and once again she has given in to the awful hope, but not any more.

Gilmore is right. Her happiness shouldn't rest on the love of others, and it certainly shouldn't depend on whether or not Marlea dumps Andrew and chooses her. She can't allow that. But neither can she imagine that Gilmore is the answer to her problems. She only chose him to take her mind off Marlea, but he was good with words, and she has taken those words and made him larger than life.

He will be like something ordered from a catalogue, the colours similar, but really not at all right. He'll be like the actors in a film based on a powerful novel. How can any actor do justice to a character the reader has already birthed in her own imagination, slowly, quirk by quirk, over the course of three hundred pages? Too many details in the acting are different. Qualities loved are gone. Attributes never considered are suddenly all too visible.

No, it can never work. Gilmore is a character in his own book. They both are—characters in the book they have jointly written over the summer—and Gilmore could never be half the man she has imagined.

She skims through all the old journals she brought to the

Pearl Luke

tower, and she is bored by their redundancy—endless pages
charting bits of learning and an abundance of identical
regrets repeated and recorded too many times. *It's not fair*,
she reads again and again, as if someone, somewhere, had
once promised that life would indeed be fair. Some of the
writing is tight and controlled, written when she was
merely recording or describing, other bits are loose and
scrawled, the handwriting a better indication than the words
themselves of the emotion no page could capture.

She is glad that she has written nothing this week that will
add to this measure of her failure. All those years, she just
didn't get it. And now she does. There will be no more manipulative games and no more lies, not to herself, not to anyone.

She catches sight of herself in the mirror, her eyes
swollen, her hair a mass of greasy rope. Look at her. Look at
the mess she's in.

As far as Percy knows, Marlea rarely feels sorry for
herself. She doesn't need to. If she wants something, she
merely begins telling people what she wants. Then almost
magically, she says, the thing appears—a gift, an opportunity, even help, from the most unlikely places, and if nothing
happens, she is content to wait for something else to come
along, something she could never have expected.

Outwardly, Percy has scoffed. It's like prayer. If you get
what you want, it's divine intervention. If you don't, you're
simply waiting. How do you lose?

But why would I want to lose? Marlea responded, and
Percy had no reply. Her question seemed suddenly irrele-
vant, like the time in Mexico when she complained about
dogs that barked the whole night through. But why do you
listen? the owner of the hotel had asked.

Why indeed? The truth of the matter is that Percy has
always envied Marlea's approach and has even tried it

herself, with little success. For her, results are directly related to effort.

You can get whatever you want, Uncle George said, so long as you get off your butt and make it happen. Within reason, he amended. But don't be surprised if, once you get the darn thing, it looks a lot different than you thought it would.

That would only mean I didn't get what I wanted after all, Percy said.

Uncle George smiled amiably. Not usually, he said. Not usually.

Well, I don't need Marlea, Percy thinks, and I don't have to meet Gilmore. She allows this new idea to take hold, and right away she feels at home with the thought, as if she has somehow kept it handy all along, like a warm towel beside the tub or slippers by the bed.

She makes room in her mind for the disappointment she thinks she ought to feel, or even for guilt at making promises she can't or won't keep, but she feels nothing, not even relief.

Now that she has made the decision not to meet Gilmore, she has no reason to long for the end of her season, but the end of the season has arrived anyway. With the helicopter scheduled to collect her and her things on Saturday afternoon, there is only one promise, to herself, that she wants to keep.

THE cabin is a closed-in, cluttered-up mess. Percy scruti-
nizes it, unsure where to begin the chore of packing. Before
last night's decision, she had packed nothing except each of
the novels she had devoured over the summer. These she
tucked, week by week, into their crates, always waiting until
the new characters, from a new book, moved in to inhabit
imaginative space that previous characters still clung to. If
the new characters were weak or failed to move her, the
previous book stayed put on her bedside table.

She has become similarly attached to the smallest items
in her cabin—the garlic braid hanging from the cupboard,
postcards thumb-tacked to walls. Each one has helped to
stave off loneliness, and she is reluctant to move anything
that will leave only empty, alien walls.

Yet she must begin somewhere, and so from the storage
shed she retrieves a heavy apple box, one of several grocery
cartons stored from April to August. A furry brown spider
sits motionless inside. She turns the carton upside down and
bangs until the spider drops to the floor and scurries under
a stack of boards, seemingly unconcerned over its abrupt
eviction. If you're a spider, there's always another box,
another board.

Blunt-nosed voles escape before she finds them, quick
peripheral flicks in the corner of her eye. They have begun
their furtive migration under and into the shed, are already
building loose nests of dry grass to be discovered and swept
clear next spring, and she hopes the next tower person—for
Percy has already decided that she definitely won't be
returning—will look down from the tower on those vole

cities and suburbs, newly exposed by melting snow, and will feel awed, as she always has, by the hundreds of metres of byways and thoroughfares that join each tiny community.

She is not coming back. What a strange and welcome thought. She'd leave her few remaining groceries—a half-dozen cans of vegetables, jars of spices, packages of pasta—but the cans would freeze and bulge over the winter, and the next person would likely throw everything out in the spring anyway, so she tucks all the leftovers in a box.

By late Thursday afternoon, she is finished, each of her boxes clearly labelled with her name and its contents: kitchen, bedroom, books, and miscellaneous. Somehow the artifacts of this simple life will be put to use in Calgary. Somehow the pulse of the city will gain strength inside her body over the next few days, a swift gestation that will make her only an awkward urbanite, a coupler between forest and city.

Her one set of good clothes hangs alone in the closet, ready for morning. Six boxes, her suitcases, and an assortment of soft bags are also ready, stacked just inside the door. The cabin stands bleak and exposed, stripped of any character that has made it interesting, however temporarily. Now that she has gone about denuding it, Percy discovers that she prefers to leave the cabin this way after all. There is nothing left to feel nostalgic about, no hint of the happy timeless days she trundled peaceably through. No hint of the other days either, the ones she barely endured.

After evening sked, in cold drizzle, she climbs the tower, disconnects radio and speakers, gathers together binoculars and scope, lip balm from the drawer, a sheet and a few magazines from the shelf above. She squeezes all of these items into her knapsack.

From below the fire-finder she pulls an armful of white

canvas, two giant hoods she rolled and stuffed there on her first trip up the tower in the spring. She shakes them out, smooths away wrinkles, and uses them to cover both the fire-finder and its heavy wooden base. When the two protective hoods are in place, she ties the canvas around with twine so that the total effect is that of a matronly dress dummy bundled for winter. All set.

She straps the pack to her stomach. If she wore it normally, slung across her back, the bulkiness might catch on the metal rings that encircle the ladder, that provide a cage, of sorts, to prevent a fall. If the zipper, the fabric, or a strap caught on her way down, she might be strung there, arms pinned, unable to squirm free—a prisoner until set loose by the next passerby. She has imagined her bones picked clean, bleached and polished by the weather before she is ever found, so she has always been careful about turning the pack to the front. Now, as she begins the climb down, she pulls the hatch door behind her for the last time. She feels its weight pressing on her head for one, two, three steps, and then the door fits into its frame and the pressure is off. Stepping down one more rung, she reaches up and hooks the padlock.

After her descent, she makes use of what little light remains to remove the downspouts on the eavestroughs and drain the water barrels. She cleans just as carefully as if she were returning, and with rainwater she has saved in a bucket, she uses an old mop to swish the sides and bottom of each water barrel free of silt and scum. When she has finished, she rolls them over to the shed, bear-hugging each one inside, a bit at a time, into its winter position.

That accomplished, she flips the lawnmower upside down. Normally she cleans the underside with a wire brush, but as hers lies somewhere in the long grass, where she kicked it, she uses a handful of dead twigs, scrubs until they break, then repeats with another handful, and another, until the bottom is clean. Her hands are so cold they are numb, but with warm soapy water, she makes the outer casing new, then proceeds to oil the blades and all of her tools, including the shovel head, the hoe, and the rake.

She returns to the cabin, where only the computer remains unpacked. She dials her server, logs on, and checks for e-mail. There are two new messages from Gilmore, which she reads quickly.

Percy hunches over her keyboard, composing once more. In the near-empty radio room, eyes glued to the screen, she taps out a few words, reads, rereads. Deletes. She had expected the words to come easily. In fact, she labours over each one, finally erasing everything to begin all over again.

August 28, she keys into the upper left corner of her screen. Then *Dear Gilmore*. Percy smiles. Her body is not vacant of feeling after all, and regardless of her decision, his name creates a soft stirring inside that she cannot explain, but can only feel. For better or worse, he has touched her in a way she will never forget. *I'm leaving right after lunch tomorrow*, she writes, *and I'll explain why very soon. Love, Percy*

The message will confuse him, but at the moment there is nothing else she can say.

In the morning, Percy awakes before the alarm rings, springs from bed and checks out the window. Fog and drizzle still. She folds her bedding into a heavy black garbage bag, then turns the mattress on its side to prevent mice from burrowing between box spring and mattress over the winter. She has left a bowl of cereal on the counter, so she eats that and dumps the remaining milk outside. She tosses the carton into the burn barrel for later.

To avoid suspicion she must report both morning and afternoon weather, so she jots numbers and checks the sway of the trees to estimate wind speed. Seven kilometres from the east, maybe. She doesn't care, wants only to get her part over with and be on her way.

When it is Gilmore's turn to report his weather, Percy's pulse jumps at the sound of his voice, but she does not rest her fingertips on the radio speaker. His voice is the thread that has connected all the days of this season. Thousands, hundreds of thousands, of words have passed between them, but the ties that held her heart securely in place have snapped, or have at least stretched to the point where urgency is no longer an issue.

She is absorbed by last-minute details. She has already boarded up the cabin windows and those of the shed as well. She closes the propane valves and lets the burners on the stove extinguish by themselves while she turns the refrigerator and furnace knobs to off.

She takes a shower and dons her last set of old jeans, along with a T-shirt under a thin sweater. She rolls her good clothes into a tight bundle and wraps them with gauze bandages from the first-aid kit. She tells herself that she is only trying to keep the roll tight so it fits into her pack, but she knows it makes sense to have these bandages on hand.

She has given much thought to the items she will take, and the rest are already in her knapsack—six breakfast bars, a can of beans, three oranges, a bottle of water, chlorine tablets, bug repellent, a thin flannel sheet, a knife, adhesive bandages, a tube of Polysporin, toilet paper, soap, a small towel, a brush, her toothbrush, a candle, a flask of brandy, and matches in a waterproof container. Everything she could think of for a short overnight hike. She wishes she could take her cell phone, but she is barely in range now. Farther away, and down amongst the trees, her telephone would be useless. The bear spray and the flare gun she straps to her waist. She is ready.

She collects the final bits of garbage from inside the cabin and the shed, including all her old clothes—T-shirts cut short and sleeveless, Vs snipped into once-round necks; baggy slacks, torn and stained; old underwear and worn socks; smelly, grass-stained running shoes. All of these she douses in gasoline and tosses into the garbage barrel. Except for these items, and the milk carton she threw in earlier, the barrel is empty, the summer's contents dumped and buried.

She adds every one of her old journals and a bundle of printed e-mail messages from Gilmore. She pauses for a minute, then pulls the ring from her baby finger and tosses that in as well.

She stands back and lights a dry stick. When it is thoroughly burning, she throws it into the container. A great whoof of sound and heat fills the barrel. Even in this drizzly weather, licks of fire reach through air holes, and a runner escapes through a crack near the bottom. She stomps on the flame, extinguishes it easily with her rubber-soled boots. So long as they are visible, flames are like that, she thinks—extinguishable. No harm done, any number of them, unless the fire takes hold and rages out of control. With a final flick of her wrist she adds another item to the burning garbage, and while the edges of Marlea's photo brown and curl, she turns away.

Four

SHE is a half-kilometre down the cutline before she really thinks about what she's doing. Getting away was easy. After seventy-five millimetres of rain, a searing blowtorch couldn't keep a fire going, and she is, she justifies, leaving only one day earlier than scheduled.

She reported the weather at one p.m., as usual, and boldly added, I'll be away from the radio for the rest of the afternoon.

Let them think what they will; when it's this dull and wet, no one bothers to question. For all they know she wants to turn her radio off and go back to bed. Maybe she wants to read, or meditate, or play Mozart uninterrupted by the inevitable belch of radio static. Perhaps they even imagine her baking moistly fragrant whole-grain breads or struggling over long cheerless letters to friends who have half-forgotten her existence. More likely, they don't think about her at all. Imprisoned by the forest, she has nowhere to go.

Except that Percy has pored over the map, charting a route to somewhere else. She has the directions in her pocket: past the old airfield and down the cutline until she crosses a second cutline. East on that one until she meets up with the old logging road, straight until she hits gravel, then one more cutline after that and she will have arrived at the edge of the lake. Maybe she'll even be lucky enough to hitch a ride on the gravel road. If she walks briskly and keeps her pace steady, she will be there in five or six hours. Less if she can catch a ride.

Through drizzle so fine it is barely a mist, she strides along the well-worn path, wades forward through tall grass she must push aside, skirts pools of water, and steps carefully across waterlogged muskeg. Her jeans are soaked to the waist before she gets to the other side of the old airfield, and she knows now that she'd be better off in a lighter fabric, something that wouldn't hold its weight quite so relentlessly, wouldn't chafe her thighs, but she has gone too far to turn back now. It would take twenty minutes to walk back to the cabin to change, another twenty to retrace her steps, and she'd be forty minutes into the afternoon and only setting out again. Better to deal with wet jeans.

A half-kilometre farther down the cutline and her socks begin to bunch. Her hiking boots are nylon and water resistant, but already she can feel her feet getting wet and cold. She stops once to adjust her socks and tries to tighten her laces, but the boots fit poorly, and still the socks inch down over her heels, down, down, a bit at a time until each wrinkle fits like a tiny pebble under her arch. The socks are all cotton, loose at the ankle to start with, already wet and gritty. She limps over them, unsure whether to take them off or leave them on as unlikely insurance against blisters that now seem inevitable.

Tall grasses, young willows, and baby spruce are unavoidable. She brushes past, bends them down, and holds one gloved hand behind to protect herself from their whipping return, but she can't escape the water flung as each one soaks her with shake after shaggy shake.

To take her mind off her feet, she thinks about Marlea, who always wears a leather biker jacket, even in the rain. Heavy and black, loaded with buckles and zippers, Marlea wears it with dresses too, as if the excess, the contradiction of her willowy and undeniable grace, provides her with strength. Her body is an ink drawing in lengthy, slender lines. Her jacket is a lovely abomination.

Percy's practical and unfashionable anorak—waterproof, says the label—blackens and sticks to her body. Her mosquito jacket, worn over top, protects her from the incessant insects but also blurs her vision and makes the world surreal. Yea, as she walks through the valley of insects. Yea, as she walks through a Vaselined world. Just beyond the net, hundreds of mosquitoes hover and whine and mill about, drawn from the forest floor by the heat of her efforts, impatient for the smallest bite of unprotected flesh. The longer she walks, the larger the swarm. Even as she sloshes, wet and uncomfortable because of drizzle and muck, she wishes the rain would intensify. Better solid sheets of water than this fluttering and tenacious following.

More than two hours later, just as Percy begins to doubt the accuracy of her map, she comes to a definite intersection. Although this path has also grown wild with grasses and weeds, heavy clay ruts are clearly recognizable as those belonging to a road rather than another cutline. She is nearly halfway to her destination. Her clothes are soaked through, and her feet, when she leans against a tree to check, are an unfleshly white, wrinkled as colourless raisins. She wrings sand and muddy water from her socks, and as she pours a small stream from each boot, she curses herself for not splurging on a better pair.

She risks a look at her watch, fruitlessly waving her arm against mosquitoes, then tucks her glove inside the wristband and secures the Velcro fastener once again. On this trail she does not feel crowded by leaves and limbs, but can follow her road far into the distance, as far as the long hill several kilometres off, and so she walks with new vigour, tries even to run, although her heels rub inside her boots and her jeans ride low and weighty on her hips. She wants to fly over the surface, to outrun the bugs, but clay builds in layers on the bottom of her boots, forms soles as heavy as steel, and she slows to a socket-straining trudge. On she plods, on and on, over the hill in the distance, around a long-off curve and then another and another, past a place where the road has washed away, where she measures with her walking stick the depth of the water, watches as the water rises to her knees—the mud, water, and cold all one, no longer separate annoyances, but one big obstacle. After that, for a while, she removes her boots and carries them, one squeezed under each arm, thinking it will hurt less to walk barefoot than to plod along in bunched socks and boots so heavy she can hardly lift them, *squoosh*, *squoosh*, *squoosh*, each step another assault on near-bleeding heels. But her feet without boots feel fleshless and icy, attend to every pebble in the mud and find thistles in what looks to be nothing more than chickweed growing soft between ruts that Percy now stomps through, slides into, cusses, and then simply sits in, not caring about bears, or bugs, or the time that rolls through the afternoon all too quickly.

Finally, knowing it could be days before she is found if she does not go either backward or forward, knowing she can die, can get eaten alive by insects or bears, Percy picks herself off the ground and wades into a puddle where she washes the mud from both battered feet and pulls a thistle from the ball of her left. She takes a long drink of water from a bottle in her pack and stares into the distance. She has come too far to go back. She must go forward.

Eventually, true to her map, Percy comes to the gravel road, which she follows to the final cutline. She walks—staggers, really—nearly one kilometre more, then rounds a bend. There, planted solidly in the middle of the cutline, head lifted, curious, is a sight that should put her arm into immediate motion, should set her walking stick rattling as ball bearings anxiously strike steel in the hollow cap. Instead, she stops in mute wonder and stares, astounded, at a bear so unlike any other that it does not occur to her to be frightened. A brown bear, she supposes, although what she registers is a thick creamy coat, not scruffy and matted and slept in like other bears she has seen near her tower, but full and fluffy-looking, as if only recently shampooed and carefully blown dry by some elite bear-grooming establishment deep in the woods. What makes the creamy-coloured coat even more astonishing is the chocolate trim that accents ears and snout, that surrounds soft black bear eyes and covers chocolate bear paws solid and heavy with mud, somehow belying danger, as beautiful and innocuous-looking as a Coca-Cola polar bear, as an Australian koala. A bear like no other bear, and all Percy can do is stand with her eyes straining wide, walking stick still and mute at her side.

The bear takes a step forward, not threateningly, but appearing only curious, like a large, shy puppy that has not yet made up its mind whether to wag or bark. She takes a step back and begins, somewhere in the vague backdrop of conscious thought, to consider her options. Run, drop, scream. Not one of the three makes any sense. Instead, her slumping shoulders straighten, the pain in her legs disappears, and her lips spread wide in a grin that has nothing to do with fear or nervousness. She is acutely focused, yet she merely waits to see what will happen next. She has no camera, but she doesn't mind that this is a sight for memory only, just waits, poised like the bear, grinning as if at some long-lost friend whose reappearance has left her overjoyed and infinitely speechless, unable to do anything but weep tears of surprised gratitude and joy.

Then, all too soon, the bear shakes its head, as if it too is puzzled by what it has just observed, and pads forward two or three steps into the bush, leaving Percy with nothing but the sound of snapping twigs and breaking branches to convince her that what she saw was truly there. She shakes her stick at the sky. Thank you, God, she says, not stopping to remind herself, as she normally would, that God may not exist. Thank you for allowing me to see such exquisite, unexpected life. Then she sinks to her trembling knees.

It is several minutes before she becomes aware that, in addition to the strong, welcome scent of wet earth, she smells smoke. The rain has stopped, and a sickening burnt odour fills her nostrils so fully that she wonders how she could have missed it before, bear or no wondrous bear. She rises, lifts her nostrils to the scent, then walks forward with renewed energy.

When she sees the first blackened stumps, she ignores the spurs of pain in her hips and runs toward them. She trips over a burnt, exposed root and skids forward on her stomach. She sits up and is enthralled by her surroundings. Thinning trees lie ahead, and a sooty moonscape leads toward what she now recognizes as a darkly reflective lake.

Only moments ago, almost too tired and sore to move, Percy wished she could magically transport herself back to the warmth and safety of her cabin. Now filthy, covered in mud and soot, with every joint from the hip downward grinding painfully with the effort of movement, she drags herself to her feet and runs toward, not away from, the unknown.

The sky has cleared enough so that the evening sun is partially visible off in the distance, above the treetops. Dark threads of remaining cloud divide the colour, so the sky appears like glowing coals through a sooty glass. The light flickers occasionally off the lake like live flames, and Percy moves forward through the burn until she is at the edge of the water. A bit farther along, she sees what at first glance looks like another reflection of the evening sun on water, but is, finally, a bed of burning coals.

FOR Percy, there is no question that anything matters more than those burning coals. From the first time she read about Lucifer Black and his farm near Delburne, she has wanted to see for herself. At first, the desire was merely a vague interest; over the years, that interest deepened to become a conscious need, patiently stashed on a to-do list that she would attend to some day. Then over the course of this summer, with opportunity so close by, the need metamorphosed into a compulsion she had no choice but to act upon.

She drops her pack on the shore, which is indeed warm to the touch, and turns south toward the embers. The smoky odour is no longer sickening but agreeable, reminiscent of rainy mornings and occasional campfires with Marlea. The evening is cool, her clothes cold on stiff limbs, but Percy's steps are eager, if uncertain, and as she walks, she tests the ground with her walking stick, tapping lightly at first, like a blind person with a cane, and then, as she nears the coals, stabbing, poking and turning the earth before proceeding.

She is hardly aware of her legs and dragging feet, and she stumbles again. The brass-tacked point of her stick, bearing the weight of her fall, breaks through the ground, and a chunk of sooty earth opens wide. She trips into it as the ground shifts beneath her. Another larger chunk of scarred earth gives way, and suddenly she is falling, grasping at the edges of the chasm, feeling the heat of crumbling embers opening up before her hands as large portions of burned material collapse inward. With a shriek, she finds herself abruptly at the bottom of a softly glowing hollow sliding down around her.

She scrabbles first to her knees, then to her feet, as burning coals bounce off her clothes with the slight sizzle of something red-hot meeting fabric soaked through. At last she is securely upright, her own breathing loud in her ears, her feet careful, her entire being poised for the possibility of more ground giving way.

She should have been more careful. Several of the articles in her scrapbook describe how, when exhausted coal is reduced to ash, or scoria, the ground above will crack and slide into burning pits, leaving craters the size of cars and crevasses like fault lines along an otherwise flat landscape. Percy knows this, had even meant to prevent just such a fall with her tentative stick-poking, yet somehow, even with the coals burning in front of her, she failed to connect this reality with stories collected over the years.

She lifts her feet carefully. For the first time all day they are warm, and now the soles of her boots are melting. The air is further polluted by the acrid odour of burning rubber, and she can feel the gluey stickiness of reluctant sole being left behind as she raises each foot. Her wet clothing and leather gloves have protected her until now, but her mosquito jacket has several burn holes, and she is not likely to fare as well in a second tumble. Quickly, in an attempt to work her way out before the sun sets, she kicks aside embers and scrabbles toward the edge of the pit. She has only fallen about four feet, can see cool water less than ten metres away, yet when she tests her gloved hands on the rim that holds her captive, the edges are soft and hot; they crumble when she pushes.

Christ, I'm going to die, she thinks, and her mind swirls in a kaleidoscopic panic of real possibility. Her boots will burst into flame, and then her jeans, and she will be roasted alive, while her screams—shrill echoes that resound beyond the lake and off into the forest—are heard by no one at all, only small animals, birds, and game. If she got lost, she had thought, she might start a fire to make finding her easy, but now she will be the fire, and no one will ever know because she will be cremated on the spot. Or perhaps they will know, will track her footsteps to the edge of this pit, where someone will eventually point to some small piece of bone or metal and say, *That looks like part of a human femur, doesn't it?* or *Isn't that the clasp of a zipper?*

There must be something she can do besides stand here, lifting her hot feet faster and faster, dancing on the coals to the wild drum of her heart as steam rises from her clothes and she tries to think of some way to escape the glowing pit she has carelessly, stupidly, fallen into.

Then she remembers her walking stick, which she lost when she fell, and she looks for it now, knowing that if she can find something to dig with, she has some hope of not roasting in this cavity like dinner in the oven. Carefully inspecting the coals around her, she locates the iron end and reaches for it. The end is too hot to touch, even with her gloved hand, so she shuffles her feet until she finds the wooden staff. The carved stick is broken, one end searing hot, the other charred through. But she grasps the portion in between, and holding the remains high above her shoulder, like an Olympic runner bearing a torch, she moves to the darkest end of the trench—the end with the fewest burning coals.

Again and again, like a miner with a broken pick, she strikes the burning wall, kicks each newly fallen chunk of coal until she has created a gradient that will allow her to jump out, if she can run upward long enough to gain momentum. She stops pounding and kicking and takes a run. With her first step, her leg slides through the coals and is trapped there, her wet jeans no longer protection from the heat but a direct conduit to her skin. Yelping, she falls backward and shakes her leg free, then rolls upward again in a sudden rush of adrenaline and rage. Straight at the wall she runs, recklessly bashing out with her iron-ended stick, over and over until, with a final swipe, her stick meets solid ground and falls uselessly from her hand. Once more she rushes at the wall in an attempt to springboard herself to safety. This time, as her hands push down on the rim of the pit, the earth holds and she lunges forward, her belly sliding up onto the stable surface, only her legs flailing ineffectively behind her. With a quickness only possible through unbridled terror, she rolls to the side and frees her arms, using them to push off and roll again, this time far enough away that she is able to lie on her back, hearing nothing but the sharp rasp of her own breath and the gentle suck of water kissing the ground a few metres to her left.

PERCY'S arm is shaking uncontrollably, but she lifts it to shield her eyes from the sun reflecting off the lake. To the east, dark frayed clouds still scatter light rain, and off in the distance cumulonimbus clouds—anvils flat atop billowing mounds—discharge trembling forks of lightning. It is only seven-fifteen, which means she was trapped for five or six minutes at most. This is a fact she can scarcely believe but accepts with relief because it means she has at least an hour before it will be too dark to see.

Lying here safe, when only moments ago she thought she was done for, Percy feels suddenly ashamed of all the times she has wanted to die, has considered suicide. Didn't she know, somewhere deep inside herself, that her life, regardless of how little she has accomplished, is worth saving?

Someday, perhaps unwittingly, like the bear she saw earlier this evening, she too will spark an unprecedented moment of deep gratitude in someone—simply by being alive, by standing in place offering a look, a touch, the right word, some innocuous act at exactly the moment it is needed most. What if she really could make a difference to someone, or already has? How could she ever have been so naïve as to think, even for a moment, that her life was hers to discard like some shabby outer wrapping?

She checks the sun, a dying red ember scarcely visible now, and stays as close to the shore as possible as she walks back for her pack. She hasn't eaten since morning, and her stomach clenches and growls with emptiness. She opens a can of beans and eats all of the contents, then buries the can.

The lake scoops outward, and Percy arcs with it, the beach

pebbly and sandy where she sinks down to remove her boots and socks. The soles of her boots have holes burned clear through; her heels are a mess, her every muscle screams in pain, and minor burns have left searing welts on her ankles and legs.

She undresses to her underwear and walks back to throw her filthy clothes into the burning pit. She waits a minute or two, wanting to see them flare into flames, but they are still damp and do not immediately catch, although her mosquito jacket, ruined beyond use, shrinks and melts like processed cheese over the other items.

The air is cool, and although the heat of the embers warms her, this is no time to be standing idle. In her pack is a bar of soap and she takes it to the water's edge, where she is surprised to discover that the lake is also warm, the bottom sandy and clear. She walks in, then strips out of her underwear, lathering until both she and her laundry are scrubbed clean. She dries with the small towel, then attends to her heels with Polysporin and bandages before she dresses in her clean T-shirt and jeans. She lays her wrung-out underwear beside her on the beach, hoping that the heat of the earth is enough to dry it by morning, and when at last she wraps herself in the sheet and stretches out on the warm sand, the sun has set and the embers flicker faintly in the dark.

Sleep does not come immediately, and Percy revisits the day, so eventful that it now seems like three days in one. The blue-black universe, slit with stars, provides a ceiling above; the ground beneath her is as warm as an electric blanket. She notes with surprise that the sounds hidden within the darkness do not cause her ears to strain or her breath to leap out in shallow gasps. No longer on the edge of the elements, but among them, she feels as if she has curled into the warm, benevolent belly of the earth. Effortlessly, she recalls a line by William Blake: *Roses are planted where thorns grow,/ And on the barren heath/ Sing the honey bees.* From *The Marriage of Heaven and Hell*, she recollects, amazed that both the line and the title should slip forward through time so easily.

As a student she enjoyed Blake, quoted him in papers, even scribbled some of his proverbs in her notebook, but she hadn't consciously memorized anything. And yet, unbidden, the words have risen within her, as if she has only to lie in the open air and breathe them in. *No bird soars too high, if he soars with his own wings.* And quietly, melodically, as if someone were reading aloud to her: *Those who restrain desire, do so because theirs is weak enough to be restrained.*

Slowly, with effort, her mind nudges these last words apart. They hold meaning for her, if only she could concentrate. She is more comfortable on the ground than she would have thought possible. So warm she could stay here forever. She blinks sleepily up at the sky. *Those who restrain desire.* The way she has. Hasn't she? For even while seeming to give, hasn't she always held back, wanting more, settling for less, because she is afraid to face her own fear that perhaps no one will love her the way she wants to be loved?

The stars are flicking on and off, a million lives warming the universe. *He whose face gives no light, shall never become a star.* She has been pretending light, while offering partial shade. *Excess of sorrow laughs. Excess of joy weeps ...*

She sleeps for nine hours, then wakes at six o'clock to a clear blue sky, her body bruised and stiff, but still curled warmly in the flannel sheet. She has dreamed about Marlea again, and under the bright eye of the new day, she lies on the beach, trying to recapture the dream.

She was in her cabin at the tower, and she was so tired her entire body ached. Both Marlea and Gilmore were with her, and she was showing them around the cabin. But after they'd seen the three rooms, she took them outside and up a ladder to a room in the attic. When they squeezed past all the rubble at the entry, they were surprised to see a large room, plentifully furnished with brightly painted furniture—Mexican furniture—woven rugs, and even a stone fireplace in the corner. Then Marlea looked through a doorway on the far side and asked whether this other room was Percy's too, and of course it was, even bigger than the first, a bit dusty but filled with valuable art and antiques, leather chairs, books, a Tiffany lamp.

Through the back was yet another doorway, and another. Every room was different from the rest and so large that she and Marlea and Gilmore all moved freely, with plenty of room to spare. They found a kitchen too, bright with glass blocks and colourful tiles, huge refrigerators and fabulous meals already prepared. Percy couldn't believe her good fortune at having so much space where before she thought she had so little.

It was this feeling of surprised satisfaction she woke to, and for the first time Percy realizes that she is no longer angry. Not at Marlea, and not at Andrew. She is not even angry with herself. For once she is completely happy to be alive, and she knows that whatever happens between Marlea and Andrew in the future, she has not been cheated by their love. Andrew's only crime has been loving Marlea as much as Percy does, and Percy resolves to apologize to him the first chance she has. The problem was not that they both loved Marlea, but that Percy refused any possibility that included

Andrew—as if love could be forever contained in paired boxes, every relationship as straightforward and conventional as those of their parents. Percy catches herself and laughs. As if her parents' relationship were straightforward.

She rises stiffly to her feet and hobbles forward a few steps before she gains her balance. Her underwear is where she left it, and each piece is warm and dry, despite the cool air. She swims in the lake, which is as warm and soothing as bathwater but colder farther out. The water loosens her limbs somewhat, and when she has finished, she shakes her flannel sheet out on the beach and stands on it to dress herself.

She wonders if Uncle George had a happy life. She thinks that because of his nature, he probably did overall, and wishes again that she could have known him better, longer. She sees him in her brother's face, now that Bobby has gotten older, but she hasn't talked to Bobby about him since the funeral and has given up on the idea that they will ever discuss him openly. She is content with the memories she has of them all together, and with the one framed photograph that her mother gave her after his death—the one showing Uncle George and Percy's mother sitting on a bench by the lake.

Here you go, her mother said when she gave Percy the photo. I know you always liked this picture. He introduced me to your father. She paused, as if she were deciding something, then she surprised Percy by continuing. We were together once, George and I. Her eyes brightened when she spoke of him, but quickly flattened again. I always thought it was us who'd be married, but it didn't turn out that way. I got pregnant with Bobby, and George got scared. He ran off for a bit. By the time he came back, your father and I were already married.

Percy was barely breathing. Does Bobby know?

Her mother nodded. He always hated him for it, but George was young. He was just young.

What about me?

Her mother nodded.

But why? Why didn't you and Uncle George—

Your father needed me. He still needs me. He always will. Besides, George ran off. Your father didn't.

Percy cried then, but her mother shushed her. You've got nothing to be crying for. George would've been a lousy husband and a worse father. He knew it too. He was a good-time Charlie, that one. All the same, I loved him.

Her eyes flashed and she straightened up, the conversation clearly over. There's no need to talk about this to anyone either. I've had more than my share of trouble over it all. Do you understand?

Percy did. She understood all too well what guilt and gossip had done to her mother, and she would spare her any way she could. How her parents' marriage had survived was difficult to fathom. Had anyone asked her, she would have said that it was her mother who had always been preoccupied with morality, but she can see now that, regardless of their sins, they were both equally virtuous.

Her parents are in their sixties now and as they always have been, yet they are different too. Both of them receive an old-age pension, and the trailer of Percy's childhood has been replaced by a small house. They are slower to slide their chairs out at the table, quieter when they eat, content to let Percy fill in the spaces while they nod and chew in silence, only her mother asking the occasional question.

The last time she visited, Percy patted her mother's hand. I'm glad you're happy, she said. I'm glad everything is okay for you and Dad.

Well, why wouldn't it be? her mother responded, but Percy just shrugged.

No reason, she said. I'm just glad you're happy, that's all.

The whites of her mother's yellowed eyes watered abruptly. We've got a lot of years left in us yet, the good Lord willing. She turned her hand over, and as if to prove it, her fingers were strong as they squeezed Percy's.

You're a good kid, Percy. You always were. I know I don't say this as often as I should, but you're my daughter and I love you. I love both you kids. She motioned toward the living room to include Percy's father. We did the best we could with what we had, and you turned out real good. I'm proud of you.

Percy waited respectfully, and when nothing more was forthcoming, she pushed her chair away from the table and bent to kiss her mother's cheek. That's just what I needed to hear, she said. I love you too.

Now Percy sits barefoot on a blackened stump to eat her breakfast alone. She realizes that she has never given her parents a single carving. Once, a few years back, she tried to give them a figurine carved from the oddly feminine curves of a darkened, withered root, but her mother had screwed her face into a puzzled frown and said, What's this supposed to be?

Hurt, Percy had snatched her carving back. Even when her mother tried to explain, saying, It's unusual, that's all, I didn't know what it was, Percy remained obstinate. If they couldn't appreciate her work, they didn't deserve to have it.

Now she wishes she had given them something else, something they *could* appreciate. She picks up bits of weathered wood along the beach. In some she sees shapes, in others she does not, but somewhere on this beach is a piece her mother will like.

Percy looks at her watch. Her original plan had been to take a good look at the site of the underground fire and to walk back this morning, fresh after a night's sleep under the stars. She wouldn't have arrived at her tower until noon at least, and she would certainly have been reprimanded, perhaps even fired, for causing everyone concern. But walking back is out of the question now. The joints of her body are locked into painful stiffness, and her feet are too sore to wear shoes—supposing the soles of her hiking boots aren't melted into hard black donuts of rubbery plastic.

Last night, when she didn't answer her call for seven o'clock sked, the duty officer would have been notified, people would have worried, but no one would have panicked. It was the night before her tower closed, and in the bustle of packing and cleaning she could have turned her radio down and forgotten the safety call. Only much later in the evening, when she didn't notify anyone to apologize for her oversight, would everyone begin to worry in earnest. Still, given the expense of a helicopter, given the fact that it would be dark already and unsafe to fly, the duty officer would have done nothing until morning.

But it is six thirty-five. Already the concerned duty officer, along with her own supervisor, will be on the radio trying to reach her. When they are unsuccessful, they will call for the helicopter—previously scheduled to haul her and her belongings out in the early afternoon—and both forestry officers will fly to her tower early. They will see her gear already packed, and their anxiety will escalate.

She is counting on Gilmore to guess where she is, and when they find her, a reprimand—now that she thinks about it—is out of the question. After seven seasons, she will certainly be fired.

She eats one breakfast bar and an orange. Her stomach is

rumbling, and she is hungry enough to eat everything in her pack, but to be safe she will make her supplies last. She looks behind her. With all the vegetation gone, there is little threat from animals, and now that the sun has returned, she will be comfortable on the beach.

She wishes she had brought a book to read, but she has her knife, and already she is eyeing a particular piece of scarred black wood, incorporating its charred edges into the smoky shapes forming in her mind. If she's quick, she may be able to rough out a simple carving before the helicopter arrives. She will call it The Marriage of Heaven and Hell.

Acknowledgments

I wish to thank many people for their advice and support during the early drafts of this novel, particularly Aritha van Herk, for without her direction and encouragement I may never have begun the work and certainly would not have finished it. Thanks also to my agent, Denise Bukowski, for finding the right publisher and for the title, which finally works. Thanks to B. J. Wray for emotional and intellectual support, to Nicole Markotic, and Suzette Mayr for early edits; to Miriam Grant for positive comments when I needed them most; to Jude Polsky for fire tower advice and friendship; to Rebecca Walsh, Denis Yunker, Terri Boyle, Lyn Goertzen, and Bonnie Burchat for later responses and encouragement; to Marie Davis for close readings, insight, humour, and invaluable discussions; to Karen Grant for information on underground fires; my fellow writers and also my friends for love, support, and eagerness, particularly Ken and Mich Rivard, Phil Hoffmann, and Cheryl Baldwin. Many, many thanks to my editor and publisher, Iris Tupholme, for her cheerful approach, as well as for her insight, wisdom, and guidance; thanks also to Karen Hanson and Lorissa Sengara for further insight and accuracy. Finally, I am especially grateful to my daughter, Amanda Ziola, for her feedback, love, and championship, and to my partner and best friend, Robert Hilles, who has aided and encouraged me in every way imaginable.

The author gratefully acknowledges support provided by the Alberta Foundation for the Arts and by the Canada Council.